MANDY
WHO's YOUR
DADDY!

NIXON

A FOUR SONS STORY

KER DUKEY

Nixon

Copyright © 2018 Ker Dukey

Cover Design: All By Design
Photo: Adobe Stock
Editor: Wordnerd Editing
Formatting: Raven Designs

I am devious, a dark soul, and son to a dead man

—or am I?

I plan many moves ahead to get the result I want.

Her.

Things may be complicated, but we were always

destined for each other.

I'll protect her from any threat and defend my interests,

even if it means going against my own brothers.

My name is Nixon Pearson.

I'm ruthless and deadly, but also devoted.

People may think I'm young and naïve,

but that's just a mask I wear to fool them.

Author Note

This novel contains some scenes that may be triggers for the

sensitive reader.

Please read with caution.

DEDICATION

For all my dark bitches.

Normal is for the mundane.

FOUR FATHERS RECAP

(For those who have not read the Four Fathers Series)

Rowan, a beautiful young woman, just turned eighteen and is friends with the four Pearson brothers next door. Hayden nineteen, Brock seventeen, Nixon sixteen, and Camden fifteen.

Rowan briefly dated Brock, had a teenage crush on Hayden, and is best friends with Nixon. But when Eric Pearson, their father, sets his sights on her, she allows him to seduce her.

Eric Pearson is a wealthy and successful businessman whose wife supposedly ran off many years ago. He likes to play with things that aren't his and when he begins an illicit affair with the teenage daughter of the single father next door, he has no idea he's taunting a dangerous man.

Jaxson Wheeler is a serial killer. The only thing precious on this earth to him is his eighteen-year-old daughter, Rowan. So when he believes Rowan has been corrupted by Eric, he knows Eric needs to die. And by his hand, just like Eric's wife did many years ago unbeknown to anyone but Jaxson.

Jaxson abandons his plan to kill his latest mark, the girlfriend of one of Eric Pearson's business partners and best friend, Trevor Blackstone, and instead seeks revenge by killing Eric and leaving him in the same grave Eric's wife has been buried in since her disappearance.

Angered by his daughter's betrayal, Jaxson flees only to return seven months later to take a trophy of his own.

ONE

N I X O N

Nineteen...

Am I a psychopath?

TOUCHING THE SPINE OF THE BOOK, A LAUGH TUGS up my lips. What a title for a psychiatrist to have on her bookshelf. *Am I a psychopath?*

I've asked myself this question many times, but never thought buying a book would give me the answer.

We all have psychopathic tendencies. If you strip back the traits and dive into the essence of your core, the parts that make up the foundations of who you are, what makes you, you—they're there. They're in all of us to some capacity.

Am I a psychopath?

It's a question everyone could ask if we broke it down to the basic facts and stripped ourselves back to reveal the whispering behaviors we try to ignore—we pretend don't exist.

The question we should ask, however, is how many of these traits exist within our minds? How consistent, persistent, are these qualities? The reason behind them and how they manifest in situations is forced upon us, separating the psychopaths from the "normal" people.

"Does that title interest you?" Dr. Winters asks, taking a seat and placing a glass of water in front of her on a table—a table that will separate us as soon as I sit on the couch opposite her. I hadn't realized I was still touching the book.

"I asked someone this question once," I say, brushing my fingers across the other titles and then pretending to dust them off. After coming here for over two and a half years, I know there's never a thing out of place or a speck of dirt in her office. She's a clean freak.

I squint my nose in distaste just to watch her eyes widen and dart to the bookshelf. Seems I'm not the only one in this room with issues. I walk toward her and push the glass of water to my side of the table before moving over to take my seat. She didn't ask me if I would like water—she's become used to me declining—but it's our last day, and I want to mess with her a little.

"Whom did you ask?" she queries.

"Is that important?" I pick up the glass and take a deep swig, the ice-water chasing the dryness from my throat.

"If they matter to you, it matters." She smiles...almost.

"Do you want to know what they said?" I arch a brow and wipe my lips. Her eyes follow the movement.

"Do you want me to know?" Her voice is calm, like her words are spoken through a silk cloth. It's a trick to get me to trust her.

"He asked me a question in return," I inform her, leaning back with my hands behind my head. I lift my feet and cross them at my ankles on her table.

Her eyes flinch when a piece of mud from my boot drops in the glass and floats on top of the water.

"Do you want to tell me the question he asked?" She straightens and shuffles her ass back.

"If I killed someone you love, would you care?"

She tenses, but it's fleeting. "Is that a question or the answer?"

I smirk. "That's the question he asked me."

"And what was your response?" She tilts her head, studying me.

"I didn't have one at first. He said if I was searching the sea of people I love in my mind, then I'm probably not a psychopath."

"So you got your answer," she concludes, crossing her leg over her other thigh. Her skirt rests just above her knees, giving me a brief glimpse of her panties from the movement. I'm not sure whether it's deliberate, but I also don't care. I narrow my gaze on hers.

"But what if I don't love anyone?" I ask, leaning forward. "Is the answer the obvious one?" I smirk.

Her hands tighten on her notepad. "That doesn't make you a psychopath."

I keep my eyes trained on hers, holding her gaze.

"Doesn't it?" I frown, holding back my grin when her eye twitches. She's never been able to figure me out.

And I don't need her to answer that question. I already know the answer is yes.

Yes, I would care.

I'd care a whole fucking lot.

Because I do love.

I love her.

And that's why I had to kill *him*.

TWO

N I X O N

From the beginning...

#1 Trait of a Psychopath

Fearless

SOUNDS OF ALL THREE OF MY BROTHERS' LAUGHING together carries down the corridor to my room. Irritation flares inside me as I jump up from the bed to close the door.

I want to shut them all out. I hate how they just accept our dad is dating a girl we grew up with. A girl barely fucking eighteen. A girl who isn't meant for him. I may only be sixteen, but in our case, age doesn't matter. We belong together.

I wear a mask of indifference, not letting it slip that I

actually give a shit. Rowan affects us all.

We knew there would be competition between us for her affection, but Christ, none of us could have foreseen our father parading her around as his play thing.

She broke my fucking heart the day I saw them together. I thought she was different than other girls. She didn't care about money, power, or looks. She liked to laugh, play around, eat pizza, and order her own fries instead of stealing mine.

She didn't beg for attention or need compliments to sate her ego. Vanity isn't something she possessed, despite being the most beautiful girl in any room.

I longed to be the one to kiss her lips. Hold her in my arms and protect her from the harshness of the world. I longed for her to take away some of the cold darkness inside me and shine her light in. She and Brock had a puppy thing going for a while, but it wasn't real—it wasn't what *we* shared.

Her being with Eric is a nightmare that keeps

me awake at night. The thoughts of him ruining her, intoxicating her mind and turning her into the troubled woman my mother became, makes me want to take a knife to his chest and carve out his heart.

I want to take bleach to my eyes and scrub away the images of them together. Hearing her moan and call out for him—*for fucking him!*—hurts. It's a pain I have to push down and mask. I don't let them see the damage they cause to me. There's always been a disconnect between Eric and me. My brothers call him Dad, but he's never been a dad to me. Even saying the word reminds me of him forcing Rowan to call him Daddy. Makes me sick. And knowing him, how bad I have it for Rowan would just make him rub it in my face more. He loves letting everyone know he's doing disgusting things to her.

I can't believe the performance he put on at the party earlier in front of everyone. Making Rowan tell her father she had a new daddy now. It almost had me exploding in a fit of frenzied rage, but I kept it together, biding my time, slipping my easy-breezy face into place for all to see so they don't know what's happening inside my mind. No one can figure me out, and that's how I like it.

Patience serves me better. This is the long game. Her own father, Jaxson Wheeler, isn't one to be made a fool out of, and why lay myself out there when I know he will deal with my problem for me?

Eric pushed his luck too far tonight. He thinks he's untouchable, and to most people, maybe he is. But Jaxson Wheeler? He isn't most people.

Eric forcing Rowan to tell her own father she doesn't belong with him anymore was him signing his own death warrant.

The whole scene made me want to vomit. Rowan's father isn't someone to just be told what is what. He makes his own rules, and I admire that about him. I've watched him over the years—watched him watch everyone else. Like me, he wears a mask. He hides his true face, and that intrigues me.

He tries to fit in, but under the surface, he sees everyone but Rowan as irrelevant. I've searched his eyes and found the stone cold entity lying behind them.

He looked inside me too, wading through the darkness with a searchlight to get a reaction. A truth. He wants to know if Eric and Rowan being together bothers me. He wants me to take his bait and do something about it. But why show my hand when I know he'll do the dirty work for me?

Fuck, I'm sick of feeling this shit—sick of letting her consume me.

Checking my cell, I sigh at the six texts from Jackie, a girl from my school who wants me to date her. She's needy as fuck. I hate her.

I don't bother replying. She'll get the message.

My eyes just close when I hear screeching. *Rowan*. I'd know her voice anywhere.

I dart upright and listen. Maybe I was dreaming. I can still hear a faint hum from my brothers in the house.

Just when I'm about to drop back onto the pillow, the dull sound of voices filter through the pelting against my window. Getting to my feet, I peek out the window. If Eric is out there doing shit with Rowan, I'm going to hate myself for getting up to witness it.

I search the darkness, but don't see anyone until a flash and the crack of a gunshot echoes through the air.

Thud.

My heart stops, then begins to thunder against my ribcage.

Fuck.

My feet are moving before my mind has even caught up. I take off running through the house, jumping the stairs three at time.

"What the hell was that?" my brothers call from somewhere in the house, but fuck them. I need to get to Rowan.

The rain is thick and heavy, drenching me within seconds. As I enter Wheeler's yard, my feet slip in the wet mud.

The rain is insane, making seeing them clearly almost impossible.

Squinting through the torrent, I make out Jax Wheeler with a gun outstretched in his grasp, aimed and ready. He's growling down at...Rowan. She's in a heap on the grass, her clothes glued to her skin, her hair stuck to her face, features etched into agonizing pain. She reaches forward toward something in the ground.

"I never should have cut you out of your mother," he spits down at her.

I react to her sobs, to her sounding so broken, and move forward to see what she's looking at. It's a grave-sized hole that's been dug in the ground. I follow her vision, and the air whooshes from my lungs. Eric is wide-eyed, staring up with a bullet hole in his skull.

Fuck.

He did it. He killed him.

I knew he would.

Charging forward, I collide with Jaxson taking him to the ground. His body crashes with a splutter into the mud. Because that's what any son would do.

Rearing my arm back I land a punch to his jaw, but he throws me off him, using his size to gain control over me, then he aims the gun at me with a sick smirk on his lips.

Thud.

I dart forward, despite the danger. I may be smaller, but I'm faster, and there's this weird adrenaline making my choices for me. I'm not scared; I'm excited.

Hitting his hand so it's not aimed at me, the gun shatters through the night, firing off a round. *Motherfucker*. I jump on top of him, trying to land another blow, but he smacks me in the nose with the butt of the gun, stunning me and making me fall back. He rights himself with ease. Wild eyes track my movements.

Warm rivers of blood mix with the rain as my nose leaks. I grin back at him when his eyes flash wide and drop to Rowan.

What's that look right there? Fear? Regret?

A commotion ensues behind me when my brothers all race into the yard and over to Rowan.

I don't want to take my eyes from Jaxson but their sudden anxious pleas for her to stay with them steals my attention.

"It's going to be ok, Ro, don't you fucking die on us."

"Call an ambulance"

"Stop the bleeding"

The rain is punishing and it takes me a few seconds before I see the blood.

My insides collide, and my hands shake. She's bleeding. Fuck. Fuck. No.

A cracking sound splinters the air and I'm not sure if it's thunder or my chest splitting open. My feet are moving to her side trying to keep this panic inside me from ripping free and swallowing me.

I need to be calm, she needs me to be calm. "Move." I bark, pushing Hayden out the way and running my hands over her stomach. Ripping the material of her shirt to expose her skin I inspect the wound. A small red hole the size of a cent oozes her essence soaking my hands. Cam rips his shirt off and hands it to me to place over the seeping hole.

"An ambulance is on its way. Is she breathing?" Brock asks relaying the situation to someone on the other end of his cell phone.

Cam is by my side squeezing Ro's hand. I survey the position of the wound on her stomach. It's low, and to the right of her organs. "Check for an exit wound," Cam tells me, lifting her a little so I can check her back. Nodding in agreement my fingers feel around her skin on the back of her hip and I feel it, an exit wound. A sigh passes my lips as I nod at Cam and he gives me a reassuring smile in return. "That's good," he encourages. I've watched enough cop shows to know a through and through is a good sign. Ignoring the panic in Brock's voice as he tells the operator there's a lot of blood, I search the yard for

Jax and catch the glimpse of him just as he slips out the gate.

Reaching for Cam's hand and placing it on the shirt so I can free up mine, I wipe my hands on my soaked shorts. "Take care of her, Cam," I urge my younger brother and I dart up, giving chase.

My feet slap against the asphalt, shooting a sting up both legs, but it doesn't slow me down. The fucking old man is fit as fuck.

After a few minutes, he slows to a stop and turns to face me. He's not even out of breath. There's no emotion in his vacant stare—no remorse or fear, the brief glimpse of emotion moments after the gun fired into Rowan has been completely replaced with indifference. I mimic his features, and it's like looking into a mirror. He's my reflection, and that's a scary thought.

Could I kill someone? Is my soul that black?

"I don't want to kill you," he tells me, and I believe him. There's sincerity to his tone.

"You shot Rowan," I bark. "She's your damn daughter." He needs to be reminded of this.

"She caught a stray bullet. I only wanted Eric." He shrugs. Un-perplexed.

"He's my father," I growl. "You think I won't avenge him?" I tilt my head, studying him.

A cocky smirk lifts his lip. "You don't give a shit about him. And we both know he's not your father. Perhaps you should ask Uncle Trevor if he knows who your real daddy is."

Bastard.

My brow furrows at his words, but I choose to ignore them for now.

"If she dies, I'll come for you," I warn instead, and I mean it. I may only be sixteen, but that won't stop me from avenging her.

"You love her?" he asks, amused and curious. Like the question is one that surprises him. He sees the reflection, just like me.

The night sky cloaks us in its shield, and out of all the people in the world, I feel like Jaxson may be the only one who understands me.

"I feel things for her, but we both know we don't love anything," I say, urging him to confirm it.

"Take care, Nixon. Don't make the mistakes I did," he warns me.

And then, he fades into the rain.

THREE

R O W A N

#2 Trait of a Psychopath

Cunning

AGONY.

That's the only word I can think to describe the pain I'm in. Grief is a hurt deeper than any physical pain. It's a fist clenching your heart and burning your soul, over and over. I'm searching for peace, a place to run and hide so I don't see him when I close my eyes. See his death. It feels like my skin is tearing from my bones. I just want to escape these memories. These four walls. These four boys.

I'm so alone despite the hospital room being full. All four Pearson boys sit in various chairs around my bed, and I can't mutter a word even though I'm screaming on the inside, because they lost their mother and father at the hands of mine. How can they still want to be here, to look at me?

My soul is so deflated. I don't think I'll ever recover from this. My scar is a constant reminder of what I lost—and what I didn't. The baby we created lives on inside my womb.

A buzzing of a cell phone jerks Nixon from his slumber. He hasn't left my side the entire week I've been here. Hayden stands holding up his cell phone and marches from the room to answer the call.

"Hey." Cam smiles, taking my hand in his. "How you feeling today? Ready to go home?"

I stiffen at those words.

Home.

I don't have a home anymore.

A place in the world.

"Here," Nixon says, placing a straw at my lips. He

always seems to know when I need things.

"If it's okay with you, I want you to come back to ours."

"We," Cam interjects, nodding to his brother.

"*We*," Nix continues, "want you to come back to ours. It's where you belong," he informs me. His brow furrowed as he searches my eyes for confirmation.

Emotion forms a lump in my throat, and I nod my head yes. Because where else would I go? Back to the fake life I lived before all this?

"Great. Cam's going to get your prescription from the nurse who's been giving him the eye the whole time we've been here," Nix jokes winking up at Cam who grins. "Can't help that the women love me."

"She is a woman too, she looks fifty if she's a day." Brock shivers making Cam grin harder.

"I like them with miles on the clock if you know what I mean." Cam's eyes flash with mischief causing a rare smile from Nixon.

For a brief moment their back and forth like normal makes me forget the devil I've known as an angel my whole life, robbed them of their father only a week ago.

Tears spring to my eyes and I act fast to swipe them away. Guilt eats away at me for what I've cost them.

"Ro." Brock furrows his brow and comes to sit next to me on the bed.

He's pulled away with a tug to his arm before even getting comfortable by Nixon. "She doesn't need you knocking her injury," Nixon warns in a tone that gives no room for argument. "Go pack her bag," Nixon tells him with a jerk of his head, dismissing him.

Brock stiffens, then moves past him to collect my belongings.

"I can do that," I try to tell him, but Nixon shakes his head and takes my hand.

"You need to take it easy and let us take care of you. It was too fucking close, Ro. We could have lost you."

There's pain in his eyes, and I'm not sure if he's

even dealt with the death of his father. Not one of them has mentioned him to me, or spoken about how their mother's decomposed body was pulled from a grave in my backyard.

They thought she abandoned them. Oh God, my father was a monster and I never knew. I hate myself for still loving him, but no matter how much I wish I didn't, I can't stop. He's my daddy, and I feel so broken right now. My entire being is fragmented, only held together by a thin thread.

"Please don't cry, Ro. I can't bear to watch it," Brock grunts from the other side of the room.

"Then fucking leave so you don't have to," Nixon growls at him.

Brock drops my bag and folds his arms over his chest. "What the fuck is your problem?"

Nixon turns toward him, and I swear I see Brock flinch. "She doesn't need you telling her she can and can't cry because it makes **you** uncomfortable."

"That's not what I meant, and you know it."

"Then what did you mean?"

There's a silent pause, and the air thickens before the door opens and Hayden marches back into the room. His feet falter when he sees the tension between his brothers. "What's going on?" He frowns.

"Nothing," Brock spits, twisting his face into a scowl and barging past Hayden.

He exits the room with an, "I'm staying at Ethan's," tossed over his shoulder.

Hayden places his hands on his hips and glares at Nixon, who shrugs. "What the fuck ever, we don't need him here anyway, let him be with his girlfriend."

"Don't be an ass," Cam reprimands Nixon, the dynamics are already shifting between the brothers.

Nixon hides his smirk with a hand swiping under his nose but I saw the amusement reach his eyes. His younger brother is more mature than all of us.

"Brock should be with us right now." Hayden grunts.

"He needs his best friend to lean on, we all have our own process," Cam tells him. Hayden turns his attention to me.

"Okay, Rowan, with you being eighteen now, you can choose where you go from here," he begins, but he's cut off when Nixon picks up the bag Brock dropped.

"She's coming home with us. Where she belongs."

Hayden nods and looks between Nixon and me. "Your friend is outside, Ro. Do you want me to tell her to meet you at our house?"

I can't face Suzanne right now, but she's been here every day waiting to see me. I nod a yes, and he nods in return before leaving the room.

———

Fingertips trace the shaking of my palm and I smile at Camden who flashes me a reassuring smile. The houses, side by side, look no different than how they always have. Yet everything has changed.

My heart thunders in my chest as Nix opens the car door and offers his hand for me to take.

Inhaling a few breaths, I step out, emotion clogging my throat and burning my eyes.

Being ushered inside gives me no time to change my mind and run—run away from it all and not stopping until my lungs give out and my heart ceases to beat.

"We have the maid setting you up in one of the spare rooms, but you can crash wherever you want," Camden says, sheepish, referring to if I want to sleep in his father's room.

God, I never stopped to think about it from their point of view. Everything with Eric happened so fast...a whirlwind that knocked the air from my lungs and rational thought from my mind. I was addicted to him, to being wanted by him. He was a raging fire, and he consumed every part of me. The rest of the world was just billowing smoke too thick for me to see through. I was lost in him.

"The spare room is fine," I tell him, giving his arm a squeeze. "Who's the maid?"

"Hayden hired some old woman," Nixon scoffs. "He thinks we need someone to keep the house in order."

"She can't cook, though," Camden grumbles. "And I'm starving."

I smile, and it feels so foreign on my face, I touch my hand to my lips.

"I'll get Rowan settled and then make us some food," Nixon informs Camden, who beams back at his brother. Nixon has always been a great cook. From a young age, he just knew how to mix flavors to create something delicious as a result. My father was also a great cook. My heart dips and the hollow pit in my gut spreads wide.

"Hey," Suzanne calls, letting herself in. There's pity creasing her features, and it makes the sickness burn a path up my throat. I dart down the corridor to the bathroom and empty my stomach.

Muffled voices hum in concern. I want to lock myself

away in here, but know it will be useless. They'll just seek me out.

Swiping a hand across my mouth, I click the door open and find Nixon waiting outside. I take the bottle of water and towel he offers.

"Let's get you to your room and you can rest for a bit."

Memories are in every inch of this place. It's full to the brim, and it's a special kind of torture when I get upstairs and come face to face with the giant window that looks out into both their yard and what was once mine. Clutching a hand around my stomach, I will my legs to stay standing. Police tape surrounds the yard, and there's a white tent pitched where the grave was dug.

It feels like the sun has gone down and will never rise again. Turning into Nixon's embrace, I inhale his scent and pray my heart doesn't crack.

"It will be okay, Ro. I promise."

Promises are empty. Eric made promises too. Now,

he's dead.

I pull from his grasp and move downstairs toward Eric's room. Taking a few deep breaths, I push open the door, and my lungs squeeze tight. It's just like he left it—like he'll return home from work at any moment. His earthy scent still clings to the air, and my knees finally buckle.

FOUR

N I X O N

#3 Trait of a psychopath

Ruthless

THIS IS RIDICULOUS. I DON'T NEED SOME SWEATER-wearing idiot to help me get over the death of my father—if he even was my father. It's only been a few weeks since we got to bring Ro home, and I should be there with her, not with some psychiatrist. I don't know why Trevor brought me here, like it will change anything.

I wish I could see my father one last time to ask him if he regrets poking the bear next door.

Being shot would have been a bitter pill to swallow for him, but it's probably best for him that he didn't make it out of that grave breathing.

I feel for my brothers, though. Well...Camden. He's young, and as much as I want to be a man he can look up to, the murky water in my veins worries me. What if someone pushes *me* too far? I came close once...

Walking around the room, Trevor sighs loud enough for me to turn to him and raise a brow.

"What?' I bite.

"Come and sit down," he says. "You're not even giving it a chance."

"I don't need to be here." I shake my head and throw my ass into the seat next to him.

This place has no air in it. It's hot as fuck.

Trickles of sweat bead and run down my back. I hate losing composure but the sticky air is agitating me.

I want to be at home with Rowan. She doesn't eat unless I cook for her.

Grief counselling and keeping your attendance up at school will assure the courts that Hayden is a capable guardian. Hayden is taking on a hell of a lot for a boy his age, and you didn't want to come and live with me and Lucy, so here we are," he grinds out, picking a piece of invisible lint from his pants.

His stupid sandals look ridiculous, but he doesn't give two shits what anyone thinks, so I keep the thought to myself.

He offered for Cam and me to go live with him, and although Cam could benefit with a man like Trevor raising him, it's too late for me. I don't need a father figure now. I'm grown and can take care of myself.

I wouldn't leave Rowan either. I can't. She needs me. And Cam wouldn't leave me. Eric was never around anyway so it's not like we're suddenly alone. Even when he was present, his mind was preoccupied. Nothing's changed apart from Hayden being stressed the fuck out and trying to navigate this new role he's been forced into.

"It's not that I didn't want to. It's not about you. I just don't want to leave my brothers," I lie, and it comes to easily. Our species is a disappointment to me. Tell them what they want to hear, offer a compliment here and there and they're putty.

He straightens in his seat and rests a hand on my shoulder. *Putty*.

"I know, but this is important, so just take it seriously. Please?"

"Fine." I hold my hands up in surrender and he smiles with a nod. *Putty*.

The door opens, and a woman enters. She's young. Not my young, but younger than Trevor. A tight ponytail pulls the skin on her face upward, making her eyes appear cat-like. She's pretty. A little skinny, hard edges and a flat ass, but Hayden would call her fuckable. I smirk and look her over like she's standing naked before me—just to put her on edge. Not a sweater-wearing idiot after all.

A crackling of energy zaps through my veins when a tinge of color creeps up her neck.

I don't know why, but I get a buzz knowing people are uncomfortable around me. Maybe It's fitting that I'm here to see a psychiatrist.

"Sorry to keep you waiting, Mr. Blackstone," she greets Trevor, then sits behind her desk and looks over at us with superiority.

Her eyes drift to mine after lifting from my lips and a smile tilts her own. "You must be Nixon."

"Must I?" I simper. Trevor nudges me with his arm, and I exhale.

He's annoying and I want to nudge him back, with the sharp edge of the letter opener laid out for anyone to take on the doctor's desk. Is she really that dumb? Or is it a test? I'm not here because I'm violent but surely it's risky of her to leave such an object readily available should I be. Maybe it's only my brain that sees these things. Perhaps to her it's merely to open letters and not a potential murder weapon.

"Nixon," Trevor growls low under his breath, but we're sitting three feet from the doctor not ten, both of us hear him. She offers him a tight smile.

Fine.

"Yes, I'm Nixon," I say, placating him.

"I've heard a lot about you from your 'uncle.' He's going to wait outside while we have our sessions. Are you okay with that?"

She speaks to me like I'm a child, and it angers me. She would probably have a field day dissecting why that is. I may only be coming up on seventeen, but I've been a man a lot longer than I should have been. The world is fucking ugly, and we have to grow up a lot quicker these days.

"Fine." I shrug. Trevor stands up and nods to her, then points a finger at me with a warning glare I find comical.

Once the door closes behind him, I track my gaze back to her to find her staring directly at me. "I'm Dr. Winters. Do you know why you're here?" she asks.

"My neighbor murdered Eric, my dad, because he was fucking said neighbor's kid."

She doesn't flinch from my crass words. Instead, she stands and gestures with her hand for me to join her over in the corner of the room, where a blue chair sits opposite a green couch. The walls hold framed certificates and a few pictures of Dr. Winters surrounded by other professionals all wearing fake smiles.

The room is stuffy as fuck. There's a smog in the air, and I want to tell her to open a window, but refuse to show her it's bothering me. Pulling my T-shirt from my body, I waft some air against my skin, then follow her and sit on the couch. It's softer than I thought it was going to be. I almost sink into it, making me feel small and consumed. I sit up straight and lean forward so I'm tittering on the edge and not drowning in the fabric.

"You have a lot of anger inside you," Winters states, like it's fact, not a question, but she still pauses for a response.

"Is that a question?" I ask resting my hands on my knees.

"No."

"Okay."

"Your uncle tells me you also lost your mother—"

Lost her, like she was a wallet I dropped at the mall.

"He's not really my uncle," I interrupt her.

Her eyes widen marginally. "Oh, well, I'm sorry. Would you prefer I call him Mr. Blackstone?"

"Why? Are you going to be bringing him up a lot?" I counter, and she frowns and dips her head. Her cheeks flush, and my mouth pops open a little before curling into a smug smile. Doc has a thing for Trevor. No wonder he brought me to see this doctor. It's nice to be wanted. Being wanted is an addiction. No matter how many people offer to love us, if it's not the one person we want it from, it's never enough.

"My mother left us a long time ago," I tell her, changing the subject and relieving her of her embarrassment.

"But the circumstances weren't what you thought. How do you feel since learning the truth?" she asks.

Ha. That's a loaded question. How do I feel? Numb.

"I wasn't talking about when she disappeared. She was gone long before then."

I swallow and look to the window dominating half the back wall. Greenery covers most of it from the outside, but there's a sliver of light streaming in from above. Why the fuck doesn't she have it open? She must like making her patients sweat. Or maybe she likes the clammy feeling on her skin. Between her legs.

"Do you need some water?" she asks. Is she testing me? I shake my head no.

Fuck you, I won't break.

"Do you?" I ask looking at her, dropping my eyes to her crotch and raising a brow.

Her calm falters briefly and she swipes a hand down her skirt and wipes her brow.

"What did you mean by 'she was gone long before then'?" she asks, ignoring my question.

I refocus on her face and stare her down. When the

silence hangs between us, she looks at her watch and says, "We're on your time, Nixon."

A slither of annoyance ripples through me and defiance is my first defense, showing her that opening those wounds is a dangerous game. One she might not be ready for. She has no idea I'm glad Eric is dead and was relieved to know my mother hadn't run off after all. That she wasn't out there somewhere making someone else miserable. I didn't always have this darkness inside me. My soul became tainted, murky with other people's darkness, their sins raining down over me like acid saturating me, infecting my core.

Eight years ago.... Age eight.

I've been sick for the past two days. Momma's kept me home from school, but she tells me I'm not allowed out of my bedroom because she doesn't want to get sick. I hear her through the walls. She's crying again, and I feel bad for her.

I want to give her a hug, so I gently open my door, willing it not to squeak like it usually does. The carpet beneath my feet mutes the sounds of my footsteps as I make my way across to her room. The door is open, and I can see her sitting on her bed, hands covering her face as her body shakes. She looks so small. I come up to her chin already, and I'm only eight. She always tells me she doesn't know where I get my height from, but my dad is tall, so maybe it's from him. I move toward her, and she sniffles and swipes her hands down her cheeks to dry up the tears.

"Mom?" I ask, and she stands, looking out the window. "What's wrong?"

"Do you think Mommy looks pretty today?" She turns to me and rubs the palms of her hands down her skirt to smooth out the crinkles.

"Yes," I tell her. She asks me this all the time, and one time when I told her I didn't like her top, she screamed at me and tore it off and stomped on it. She reminds me of when my little brother Camden isn't allowed a cookie before dinner.

"Well, your dad didn't think so," she snaps. "He has some new young girl working at his firm. No wonder he's always coming home late. I was that young once, and perky, then he wanted kids, and look at me!" she shouts, pinching at her tummy. I frown, not understanding. Look at what? And who cares that someone is working with Daddy. Mom doesn't have to work, and she hates it. My friends mommies like not going to work.

"I'm feeling better," I lie, hoping she'll stop pinching herself.

A noise sounds from outside, and she looks back over to the window before taking me by the shoulders and ushering me back to my room. "Stay in your room until I say you can come out." When I don't answer, she shakes me. "Are you listening to me?" My head hurts and her shaking makes the stomach ache worse.

"Yes."

She closes my door, and I listen for the echoes of her to fade. I run over to my window and look out to see Robbie *mowing our lawn. He lives down the street and Dad pays*

him to do things around the house because he's saving for

some fancy college. He sometimes kicks the ball around with

us, but he and Hayden had a falling out over Hayden kissing

Robbie's little sister. She's older than Hayden, but he still

wasn't supposed to do that with her. I saw them kissing once.

Mom says Hayden is just like our dad, but I think he looks

more like Mom. I'm bored inside my room and want to get

some fresh air. I tug at the handle for the window and frown

when Mom walks out across the lawn and Robbie smiles at

her. She rubs her hand down his chest like Robbie's sister

does to Hayden and walks over to the pool house. He follows

her, and they go inside, but I can still see them through the

windows. I frown when they kiss. My stomach feels bad again

and I think I'm going to be sick, so I rush to the bathroom.

The pain is worse today. I wish Cam didn't have to be in

school. He's younger than me, but he would bring me water

and play video games with me if he were here. When I get

back to the window, I don't know whether I should look or

not, but I don't understand why Mom would do that stuff with Robbie. I peer out again, then quickly jump back and close my curtains.

I'm only eight, but I know what they're doing is naughty and I shouldn't tell Dad.

"Nixon, do you want to tell me what you mean?"

I drag my attention from the past and focus on Dr. Winters. We've been sitting here in silence.

"Times up, Doc." I get to my feet and stride from her office.

FIVE ———————

R O W A N

#4 Trait of a Psychopath

Lacking conscience

IT TAKES LONGER FOR THEM TO RELEASE A BODY when it's a murder investigation, especially when it's someone of Eric's worth, but finally, we're able to lay him to rest. The church is full of faces I don't recognize, and I feel so out of place. Eyes from all around burn a hole into me, and I want to run. I wish I could just run. Police are here undercover, thinking for some insane reason my father might show.

The scent of all the beautiful flowers laid out for Eric hang in the air, and I don't think I'll ever smell a rose and not think of him after this.

Sickness is a feeling I'm learning to live with. I feel it constantly. I wish I were stronger for the boys who have taken care of me despite their own pain.

Brock has taken it the hardest. He doesn't come home very often and spends most of his time with Ethan, his best friend. I look over to him and my eyes close. The pain is so fresh on his young face. Tears burn my eyes as I take in the tense jaw fixed on Hayden's face. He has so much pressure on him now. I want to be able to help him, but I can't do anything.

It hurts just to breathe. Every day is more painful than the last, because I miss them...

Eric had woken the woman inside me. I was learning about love and myself, and then he was torn from me by the only other man I've ever loved. I lost them both that day.

My entire life has been a lie. The man who tucked me in at night had a monster inside him. I search every memory, trying to find a sign of who he really was, but there's nothing.

A warm hand slips into mine, and I know without looking that it's Nixon. He is my strength right now. He's always been there for me. Our friendship is one I cherish and appreciate more than he could ever know. Before things happened with Eric, I always thought I'd marry a Pearson boy.

Brock always said he would be my boyfriend until I found a real boyfriend. He said we could do all the firsts together to get them out of the way. It would be better to do that stuff with someone we know and trust, he told me. I had my eyes set on Hayden Pearson however. But then he broke my heart by kissing me and then pretending I didn't exist the next day so I agreed to date Brock, until I found a *real* boyfriend.

But Nixon...Nixon has always been my soul mate, my best friend. We go together like burgers and fries. He's never made it sexual; he just knows my soul is tethered to his and we need each other. Your soul mate isn't always the one you fall in love with. It can be a brother, a sister, a friend, even a pet. Mine is a boy next door.

We were the thunder and rain, an impeccable storm. He always shielded my heart and stuck up for me against assholes in school, but he can't save me from this pain, no matter how desperately he tries. I don't deserve him. I stole everything from him.

"Now, Eric's youngest son, Camden, would like to say a few words," the priest announces.

I watch as the boy who should be out riding his bike and swimming in the lake, laughing with his friends, stands up to speak for the second funeral this week.

He swipes his unruly hair from his forehead and looks to Nixon for encouragement. Nix nods his head and smiles tightly. Cam's Adam's apple bobs as he takes a few swallows and then speaks.

"Our dad was a proud man. He prided himself on his work ethic, and this sometimes took him away from the home, but when our mom...went away, he was all we had, and we were all he had. He wasn't perfect, but who is?" He shrugs, and a choir of sniffles sound as everyone softly hums their agreement. "He was our dad, and I'm sorry, Dad. I'm sorry we didn't get to you in time, but we want you to know we will take care of Rowan. You just take care of Mom."

My heart shatters as a tear slips from his steel-blue eyes, so like his father's. Why is this so hard?

Trevor receives him into a hug as he steps down, and gentle cries vibrate through the air, like the buzzing of a thousand bees' wings.

Nixon's hand leaves mine and he places his arm around my waist as he leans in to whisper in my ear. "It's okay, Ro. I've got you. I won't let you break."

It's too late. I broke when my father's gun pierced my entire world and ripped it apart.

SIX

N I X O N

Three months later...

#5 Trait of a Psychopath

Calm under pressure

BA BOOM. BA BOOM. BA BOOM. BA BOOM. BA BOOM. There she is, a smudge on the screen, but she's real, the heartbeat strong. A girl. Rowan is really going to be a mom to a little girl. Her hand squeezes mine and she sniffles, swiping tears from her eyes.

"You're sure?" Rowan asks the woman. The woman gets to her feet and moves the monitor over to show her what she's seeing.

She points to the screen and describes each part of

the tiny human growing inside Rowan. "Congratulations. I'll give you both a minute."

She begins printing off pictures, then leaves the room. I use a piece of tissue and wipe Rowan's stomach down from the goo they put on her, then help her to sit up. This isn't the first time she's had a scan to check things out, but the baby is more formed now and actually looks like a human midget, not just a peanut.

We've talked about a boy or a girl, but this makes it so much more real. The small rounding of Rowan's stomach makes me smile. She should be bigger at almost five months, but according to the nurse, she's carrying in her back. Whatever the fuck that means.

Her pregnancy has been good. Minor sickness and she struggles with lower stomach pain, but that's because of the wound she suffered from the stray bullet.

"So, a little Rowan running around. I bet she's going to be a handful." I wink, and she giggles, then cries. These mood swings always catch me off guard. "You're going to be great," I assure her. "You're not in this alone."

She nods her head. "I know, I know, it's just a lot, you know? I thought I'd be in college by now, not five months pregnant, living with four boys." She snorts, then her eyes widen with embarrassment. Things have changed between us lately. Before all this, her snort-laughing in front of me would have been normal, but now she's more aware that I'm...male?

"Life doesn't end here, Ro. So your path changed course, it doesn't mean you can't do all the things you wanted to do. In fact, I insist you still go to college. You're too talented and stubborn to be kept or waited on," I tease, and she bites her lip, making me want to pull it from her teeth and bite into with my own.

"I have an appointment now, but when I get home, I could take you shopping for some girl clothes?"

"You're too good at this," she breathes.

"Good at what?"

She blushes and nervously plays with a strand of her

dark brown hair.

"Being you—being what I need. I need someone on days like this, and there you always are. How did I get so lucky to have a friend like you in my life?"

The friend comment stings a little. We were supposed to be so much more than friends. He took that from me—from us.

Look where that got you, fucker.

Getting to her feet, she wraps her arms around my waist and lays her head against my chest. "Thank you, Nix. Thank you for always taking care of me," she mumbles into my shirt, and it's everything having her in my arms. I hold her to me and allow myself this moment to breathe her in.

———

The air conditioner blows through the room, turning the air icy cold.

Dr. Winters likes to play games. In the summer

months, this office was unbearable with heat, yet she didn't once turn on that fucking air.

"Are you cold?" she asks, pointing to where I'm rubbing the stupid goosebumps pebbling all over my skin. I look like a de-feathered chicken. Thanks, Doc.

"No," I lie.

Her lips twitch, but she doesn't give in to the pull of the smile.

"I noticed Mr. Blackstone didn't accompany you this time." She looks to the door, then back to me.

"He has a business to run. Hayden is being taught the ropes, so..." I shrug.

Dirty bitch is probably wishing he'd come in here once I leave and bend her skinny ass over the desk. What is the appeal of those old fuckers?

When she diverts her eyes back to the door, I exhale.

"I'm a big boy, Doc." I roll my eyes and sit back on the stupid green couch. I hate this fucking thing. It's too soft.

"Last time you were here, I asked you about the night

your mother presumably left."

I stiffen, my joints hardening and chest decompressing. She's asked me about my mother non-stop for months.

"What about it?"

"What do you remember about that night?"

Nothing. Everything. Why does she want to dissect my memories? What does she get out of this? Why can't she just go do some paperwork and let me use these sessions to catch up on the sleep I'm losing trying to keep up with school and Rowan's appointments.

"Nixon, what is it you don't want to talk about?" She stares at me like she can read my mind, and I want to shove her out of my head. She's a fucking hitchhiker on a ride she can't handle.

Six and a half years ago

Nixon

Why do they insist on throwing these parties? Why

can't we just do family stuff for once? It's like my parents can't function together unless other people are around. I hate them.

Music plays from the speakers Dad installed and they make too much noise.

I don't know why he likes to do things himself. He's always talking about how much money we have, but likes to show off.

I hate him.

Laughter fills the space, and I can't stop watching Rowan, our neighbor, as she jumps into the pool in her swimsuit. Her body is changing, and I worry she won't want to do things like build tree houses and skip stones across the lake soon.

The older girls in school only want to take pictures of themselves and wear too much makeup.

I hate those girls.

Hayden splashes me in the face, and the girl he's with this week lifts her top up and flashes me before laughing into *my brother's shoulder.*

If my eyes could set fire to her just by looking that would be so cool.

I've seen boobs before. I have a magazine Brock gave me under my bed, but the ones in the magazine are bigger than hers.

Why are the girls Hayden brings here always showing off?

"Stop staring at the neighbor, pervert." Hayden splashes me again.

Douchebag.

"I'm not." I frown at him. Why does he have to say that so loud?

I hate him.

"Your wiener is bobbing on the top of the pool." He smirks, and I quickly look down to check.

He and the girl he's with begin laughing at me.

I hate them.

He's so embarrassing. Big brothers suck sometimes. I

wish it were just Cam and me. Then maybe Mom wouldn't be so stressed out.

Mom's voice carries across the yard, like thinking about her made her appear, and my stomach drops. She's yelling at Dad in front of everyone—again.

I lift myself out of the pool and dry off before going over to where he's made her go inside the house.

They're still shouting, and we can see them through the window.

"Nix, they'll be fine, buddy," Uncle Trevor tells me, coming up and rubbing my shoulder. "Grab the football. I'll toss it around with you."

I don't want to play ball. I know they're going to be arguing all night once everyone leaves.

Maybe I can go home with Uncle Trevor?

That's not fair to Camden. He hates them arguing more than I do.

I look back to the pool to see if my little brother is in there, but he's not.

I wave off Trevor and go looking for my brother. Brock is dunking Rowan and making her scream with laughter.

"Hayden, where's Cam?" I ask, just as Rowan's dad comes over and tells her it's time to leave.

She moans, but does as she's told.

Her dad has a scary face when he thinks no one is looking. I'd do as I was told too if he were my dad.

"See ya, Rowan," my brothers yell, and she waves bye before turning to me. "Bye, Nix. Cam went inside to pee." She smiles, and my stomach flips over. She's my best friend. I don't care if my brothers make fun of me.

My dad's back outside talking with his friends by the time I make it to the house and slip inside.

I don't hear Mom crying, which is something. Perhaps she took one of her magic pills again.

A noise that sounds like a man's voice comes from the bathroom down the hallway, making me frown.

Dad opens the pool house for guests to use the restroom, so I know it must be either Mom or Camden in there, but it doesn't sound like them.

There's no reason why, but my stomach cramps.

"Camden?" I call out, pushing the door open.

I know what I'm seeing is bad—really, really bad.

There's a man in here. He's always invited to these parties because Mom says he's important. She always says he could be the mayor one day, but I don't believe her.

Mayors don't do what he's doing to little kids.

He reaches for the handle of the door. "Go to your room," he barks at me, like he's allowed to tell me what to do.

I grab the door before he can close it and slam it against his wrist with all the strength my nearly eleven-year-old body can muster.

The man lets out a weird howling sound, and the watch he's wearing snaps and falls to the floor. His wiener bounces around as he struggles to pull his swim trunks up with his injured hand.

Good.

"You little bastard," he growls. I shove past him and

grab my baby brother, pulling him with me and racing into the hallway.

The man follows us, holding his wrist.

"I was just helping him," he tells me, staring at Camden. "He's my good boy. Right, son?"

My brother trembles and lets out a terrified sob.

I've never felt a feeling like this before. My whole body is shaking. I want to take Dad's hammer and hit this man until he stops moving, stops looking at us, stops living.

I hate him. I've never hated anyone more than him right now.

I pull a crying Camden behind me and hold my hand out to signal for the man to stop moving toward us.

I don't feel my age. I feel older, and I'll do anything to protect my brother.

The man stops and flicks his disgusting eyes to my brother, who's trying to hide behind me.

"Don't look at him," I shout. "I'm telling my mom and she's going to call the police," I warn him.

"I was helping you, wasn't I?" He moves forward, and I pick up a vase from the glass table Mom has out here. I don't know why she even has furniture out here. It's stupid, and she puts these vases everywhere for no reason. I'm glad right now, though.

I chuck it at him and hear it hit his body. It then shatters to the floor, but I take off running, pulling Cam with me before he can say anything or do anything else.

Racing up the stairs and into my room, I click the lock into place and march Cam into the bathroom.

"It's okay, Camden. Mom will make him pay. No one is allowed to do this, okay?"

I wipe his teary face and help him put on some of my pajamas.

"Get in my bed," I tell him before pulling the covers back and making him comfortable. "Wait here for me, okay? Don't open this door." He doesn't argue, and I want to go back down and find that man and throw every vase in this house at him. Closing the door behind me, I head toward

Mom's room. There's a light on and sounds are coming through the door. I push it open, and my heart makes a weird flip as worry fills my tummy. "Mom?"

She gasps and puts her hand on her chest. "Nixon, you scared me."

"What are you doing?"

She's putting her clothes into a big bag. "I'm sorry, Nix, but you'll be fine."

What does that mean?

"What about Camden?" I ask. Will he be fine too?

She plays with her hair for a moment, then shakes her head.

"He has you boys. He will be fine."

She's leaving us.

"That man was touching him," I shout.

Her eyes squint at me. "What man?" She stops packing her stuff and stares at me.

"Mr. B."

She laughs and shakes her head. "Stop being silly,

Nixon. Future mayors are good men."

"He had his wiener out and was touching it while alone with Camden in the bathroom, Mom."

"Stop it!" she shouts, making me jump. "Just stop it. You can't say that about men like him, Nixon. You must have been mistaken."

How can she say that?

"Mom?" I whisper.

"Go to your room, son. And don't ever tell lies like that again, do you hear me?"

I just stare at her. I want to scream for her to believe me, love me, stay for me, but my throat dries so fast, I can't speak. Cold. I feel so cold.

She rounds her bed and grabs me so hard on the top of my arms, I know I'll have bruises when I wake up.

"Do you hear me? Don't tell lies like that to anyone."

I pull away and run back to my room, slipping into bed and holding my shaking baby brother. She doesn't care. She doesn't love us. She's leaving us.

"I promise I won't let anyone ever hurt you again," I whisper to my brother. And I mean it.

Present

"I saw her pack a bag. She was leaving us," I tell Dr. Winters.

The good old doctor nearly drops her glass at my confession.

This is the first time in all the months I've been coming here that I actually told her something.

"Did she tell you she was leaving?"

I shrug.

"How did that make you feel?"

Nice try, Doc.

Like I wanted her to meet a fate worse than what my brother went through.

Guess that came true.

My thoughts drift back to that asshole. He's big

time now. Mother was right about that much. Politics is always ran by the depraved assholes of our society. It interests Camden, and we need more people like him in the government offices. Good people.

If I ever see the fucker in person again, it won't matter how powerful he believes himself to be. I'll kill that son of a bitch.

Camden never mentioned it after that night. He was young. I hoped he was young enough to forget, but he slept in my bed from time to time until he was thirteen.

Our older brothers never knew. Perks of having a big house and self-centered family members.

"Nixon? How did that make you feel?"

Dr. Winters asks, her voice firmer. Fuck you, bitch.

"Glad," I snap as I rise to my feet. "She was useless." I wave at the clock. "Time's up."

SEVEN ━━━━

R O W A N

#6 Trait of a Psychopath

Duplicitous

A YAWN ESCAPES ME, AND MY EAR HAS TURNED RED from being on the phone with Suzanne for the last forty minutes.

"Am I boring you?" she whines.

"I just get tired easily now and I need a drink," I placate on an exhale while using my free hand to rub over my growing stomach.

"You should get one of those gorgeous boys to bring you a drink," she moans dreamily.

"You're a perv." I roll my eyes, but she can't see me anyway. She's right, however. All those Pearson boys have their father's beautiful looks.

"Anyone would be a perv for those Pearson brothers."

"Suz," I groan.

"I know, I know. They're off limits," she scoffs. "Ever heard of sharing is caring?" She snickers.

"Bye, Suzanne."

━━━━━

Hayden is making a sandwich when I come down for some water. The stairs are still a little tricky for me. Despite my injury being old, my hipbone aches and I sometimes end up walking with a limp.

I debate just turning around and going back upstairs, but the effort getting down here was too much to turn around now. Things are strained between Hayden and me. It's like there's this cloud following us around and it never breaks—never just rains down, clearing the air.

He's been dumped into the deep end over at Four Father's Freight. I want to tell him his dad wouldn't expect him to take on so much so soon, but I fear the response I'll get from him.

His eyes track mine, and his hand stops moving from slavering butter on his bread.

"Hey." He frowns, looking down at my growing stomach. I feel like I'm going to burst and still have a couple months to go.

His brow is furrowed so tight, I swear there will be a crease left there for days.

"Hey." I smile tightly. "I just came down for some water."

Pulling open the fridge he grabs a bottle.

"I thought Nixon put one of those mini fridges in your room?"

A real smile curls my lips this time. "He did, but Camden steals the drinks when he's engrossed in his video games and doesn't refill it."

Hayden raises his brow. "Nix will kick his ass if he knows."

I take the bottle he offers and laugh. "That's why I haven't told him."

"Thoughtful of you. I hope that doesn't mean you're finally moving on to Cam. A little young, don't you think?"

A gasp of wind leaves my lungs. I drop the bottle and step back when it bounces on the tile floor, missing my feet by an inch.

His head isn't screwed on right at the minute and there are things I will let slide, but this? To ever insinuate I'm making my way through them like they're desserts on a menu is cruel.

"That's a low blow." I snap my eyes up to his. He's staring so deep into me, I can't breathe. My lungs constrict, causing an ache there.

"You've toyed with us all, Rowan. Don't act innocent," he scoffs.

"I didn't toy with you," I gasp. "You didn't want anything to do with me until you thought your brother had me, and then you just didn't like him having what you thought you owned. You didn't want me," I growl.

He always told me I was too young, and then when Brock asked me to be his girlfriend, Hayden made a pass at me. It was everything I'd wanted, but I wasn't stupid. I'd been around long enough to know exactly what he was thinking and how he used girls like they were there for his amusement. My heart couldn't handle that then— and definitely not now.

He rounds the island, closing the space between us.

"That's not true and you know it." He flexes his jaw, and those glassy, intoxicated eyes narrow.

"Hayden." I push against his chest. "I'm pregnant with your father's baby."

He closes his eyes like he can't even look at me.

"Because I didn't want you?"

Wow, he's so full of himself.

"No," I step back. "That's not fair."

His eyes spring open, and there's a burning in them that makes me want to cry.

"I should never have let him have you. It just happened so fast... We failed you, Ro. We fucking failed you with him."

No. No. No.

"Stop it," I beg.

"It should have been me." He leans forward, taking my cheeks in his palms and pushes his lips to mine. My eyes expand to the size of saucers and it feels like my feet have sunken into the ground. I can't move. Shock holds me hostage and it takes me a couple of seconds to realize what the hell is even happening.

I push against his chest, and he stumbles back. Pointing my finger into him, I shake my head. "Don't ever do that again."

Liquor burns my lips from his touch.

"What's going on?" Nixon asks from the doorway, his shoulders rigid and features pulled taut.

He's shirtless, sweat coats his skin, and his damp hair is tousled, hanging down his forehead. His gym shorts hang dangerously low, and I can't help but admire the ridges of his defined abs.

No one would believe he was still in his teens. His tall, broad frame is dominating, and the atmosphere is thick as he keeps his gaze on Hayden.

"I dropped my bottle. Hayden was just picking it up for me. I'm frightened I'll fall if I bend over," I chortle to calm the air.

"Pick it up then." Nixon gestures toward the bottle still lying by my feet with his head. Hayden's jaw ticks as his eyes never leave me. Reluctantly, he picks it up and shoves it into my chest. "Drink up, Ro. You look thirsty."

Bastard.

———

"You haven't eaten much," Lucy points out. They say time heals all wounds, but I don't believe that to be true. It's been months, and it's still hard to breathe.

They haven't located my dad, which has the boys

angry and looking for him themselves. The thought of them finding him terrifies me. Hayden is so angry, he swears he'll kill him, but all scenarios lead to nowhere good.

I don't know what I want. Justice for the boys, for Eric, but what justice, prison? Death? My stomach rolls as the thoughts swirl around my mind, tormenting me.

"Rowan, you need to keep your strength up. You're eating for two," she points out the obvious, like the massive lump attached to my front isn't a constant reminder of that fact.

I appreciate the time she gives me, and we have become close since...Eric was murdered.

Trevor tries to be there as much as possible for the boys, so in turn, Lucy is there for us all too. She's fun to be around. She doesn't feel older than me, but that might be because I don't feel my eighteen years. I feel tired and worn down by life.

"Hayden kissed me last night." I vomit the words,

and she chokes on her drink. A crimson flush races up her cheeks as she coughs and sputters.

"Are you okay, ma'am?" a waiter guy asks, checking out her tits as they lift up and down with her coughing fit.

She waves a hand at him. "I'm fine. Thank you."

He walks off, and she widens her eyes at me. "What?"

I shrug. "There's always been this unspoken thing between us, but things are complicated."

She nods her head too fast, looking like one of those hula girls she has stuck on her dash. "What about Nixon?" she breathes, completely dumbfounded.

I frown. "What do you mean?"

Nixon has been incredible, he's my best friend, but he doesn't see me in a romantic way.

"I thought you and him were..." she trails off.

Me and Nixon?

"Were what?" I ask, taking a sip of my drink trying to ignore the images of him dripping with sweat last night.

"You realize he's in love with you, right?"

Now it's my turn to almost choke. She's crazy. Nixon isn't in love with me.

He's my best friend. He's too good for a girl like me.

"You're wrong." I shake my head. He's protective, but that's just because he's always been that way. It's his nature. *Right?*

"Rowan," she almost whispers.

My heart thumps in my ears. Thoughts of Nixon and I swirl guiltily in my mind. "No. He doesn't see me that way," and I've never allowed that possibility to ever enter my thoughts until right now. My stomach ignites with butterflies, and I can't stop it. No. No. No.

"He doesn't," I assure her, shaking the thoughts from my skull. I can't entertain those possibilities. Because if I'm honest with myself, the idea is just too appealing.

Damn it, why did she have to implant those ideas in my head?

"Just be careful. Those boys have been through enough. They don't need to be fighting over your affection."

Acid pours into my muscles, tightening them. "I'm not playing them," I almost shout.

The words from Hayden last night are still raw. Is that what they think? Is that what Nixon believes? Is that what everyone believes? God, am I causing friction between them? I should move out. Oh God, I can't leave them.

"I know," she placates. "It's just an unusual situation and everyone is vulnerable. It would be natural for feelings to develop and get confusing."

"I'm not confused." I cross my arms over my chest and narrow my eyes on her.

I hate that tears are forming. My turbulent contemplations are making me tired.

"What did you do when Hayden kissed you?" She bites her fingernail, a sneaky grin pulling up her lips, like we're just two girlfriends sharing gossip. I wish life were that easy.

"I pushed him away," I answer honestly, wiping the condensation off my glass with the tip of my finger. My skin feels sensitive and the flesh there tingles from the cold.

Lucy nods her head again and forks a spoonful of food into her mouth.

"There was stuff left unfinished with us I suppose, unspoken emotions that were never discussed. I don't think he meant to kiss me. I think he feels guilty about things," I offer with a shrug.

She makes an "hmmm" sound, but doesn't say anything else.

"Nothing is happening between us," I state, getting agitated.

She nods again, and I want to place my hand on top of her head to stop her from doing it every two seconds. "I mean it, Lucy. I can't."

"I know." She reaches over and rubs her palm over my arm. I relax a little, but my internal thoughts are a huge box of pandemonium.

There has always been this thing between Hayden and I, but Nixon has never pursued me romantically—and he's so different from normal boys our age. I never looked at him as someone who could be more than my best friend. I'm not blind to his appearance or the calming peace I feel when in his company, but being anything more...

No.

We can't.

And Hayden is the destroyer of young hearts. He's left a blood trail of them all through school, and now he's taken over Eric's shares of the company, opening up a whole new field for him to play in. I can't let my heart be placed in such crushable hands.

"Let's go, Rowan. School's out and we both know Nix will be worried if you're not there when he gets in." She winks at me, then pushes her plate away and rummages through her purse for money.

"He's not in love with me," I growl, but more to tell me than her. I don't mention that he's already texted me and I've told him I'm out with her.

———

Music blasts all over the house when I open the front door. Lucy dropped me off and offered to come inside, but when she saw Nixon's truck in the driveway, a stupid smile took over her face. I told her to go get laid. The last thing I needed was her causing an uncomfortable atmosphere between us all.

There's no one downstairs, so I turn down the music and freeze when grunts sound from the corridor.

My heart thunders in my chest as I move toward the noise.

Has Nixon brought a girl home with him? Does he have a girlfriend now? He hasn't mentioned a girl, and the last time he had a girlfriend, Hayden seduced her, and Nixon just shrugged it off like she didn't mean anything to him anyway.

I swallow and ignore the jealous rampage taking over my mind.

I hate Lucy for implanting this crap in my head about him.

I don't need to think of Nixon in that way. I need him too much to ruin our friendship with stupid inappropriate feelings.

The grunts turn to moans, and I almost throw up. I know he's no angel, and I could never ask him to be, but if he has a girl in here, it's still going to hurt—which is insane. I have no rights to him, nor do I even know why it would hurt. Oh God, what the hell is going on with me? My hand hovers on the doorknob to the room the noises are coming from, then I startle and almost pee myself when Nixon appears down the hallway in only a towel. My eyes go between him and the door where the moans have gained enthusiasm.

"Ro," Nix warns, shaking his head. My eyes trace the

water beading down his skin. Every muscle on his torso flexes in response, and a longing I haven't felt since Eric pools in my gut and throbs between my legs.

No. No. No. I can't look at him like this.

"Hayden," a familiar voice chants, and my mouth drops open as my stomach clenches.

Nix starts forward, but I've already pushed down the handle and let the door swing open.

Red hair covers my best friend's face as Hayden plows into her from behind. He ruts on Suzanne, bending her over an old chair—a chair dumped in here because it's trash. This whole room is used as a dumping ground, and here's my best friend being used as just that.

Hayden has always made fun of her and never shown any interest in her, and she knows he was my first crush. She knows everything, and she's allowing him to use her. He looks over at me with pure contempt, pain, and disgust pulling his features taut. I don't know if it's aimed at me, or just how he feels about what he's doing to get a rise out of me. He slaps her ass, and she gasps, then he pulls out of her and drags his shorts up his legs. He didn't even take them off, and her bikini bottoms are tugged to the side, like he couldn't even be bothered to undress her first.

She looks back at him over her shoulder, completely consumed by the moment and not even noticing me standing here.

"Did you finish?" she asks, confusion lacing her tone.

"Get out," he snaps at her.

I watch in trepidation as her shoulders deflate. Shame and embarrassment coat her in a red flush. This will haunt her. She was a damn virgin.

"Hay," she pleads.

"Get the fuck out. You're not doing it for me," he barks, dismissing her with a pointed finger toward right where I'm standing just by the door.

I close my eyes, my soul shrinking for her—for me. I know this is because I refused his advances last night.

This is my punishment. An "I'll show you."

Well done, Hayden, you've really shown me. We haven't seen this side of Hayden in a while.

Nixon grabs my wrist, drawing my attention to him. His hair is wet and sticking to the side of his face. His green eyes bore into mine, making my heart skip.

"Rowan," Suzanne gasps, and I look over at my best friend with sadness.

"I...erm...I..." She tumbles over her words, righting herself and pushing her locks behind her ears. Her brows draw in, and tears build in her eyes. Without saying anything else, she rushes out of the room, past Nixon and me.

I want to call out to her, reassure her, but she's gone before I can fathom what to say.

"You're an asshole," I spit at Hayden, who's staring at me like he's waiting for me to explode. I won't give him that.

"That's nothing new," he states. "Does it hurt?" he

asks when I drop my eyes to the floor.

Nixon stiffens next to me.

"No," I tell him honestly. It doesn't hurt; it just enforces what I already knew: Hayden would break me if I gave him the chance. Hell would have to freeze over before I ever let that happen.

"Why are you denying you have feelings for me?" he growls, marching toward me. Nixon hasn't removed his hand from my wrist, and it tightens a fraction every time Hayden speaks.

"I had a crush years ago. Get over it."

Laughter, rich from his chest, vibrates the tension in the air. "That's bullshit and you know it."

I shake my head, a laugh of my own bubbling to the surface. He's so full of himself. "You're so arrogant."

He smirks. "Remind you of my daddy?"

A wheeze pushes from my lungs.

Nixon's hand drops from my wrist, and he bows his head, like those words hurt him just as badly as they do me.

"You finished?" I ask him.

"Why? Is your lapdog going to attack in a minute?" He nudges his glance to the shadow of Nixon's form standing just out of sight.

"Why her?" I ask, shaking my head in disappointment.

"Why do you care?"

"Because she's my best friend and you treated her like shit just now."

He swaggers over to me and stands so close, I can feel his breath as he exhales.

They're too much together, this close, I need some room to breathe to keep my focus.

I step away from him, but he advances until my back hits the wall.

"Why do you really care?" he demands. My eyes drift to Nixon, and my heart hammers in my ribcage. There's this look in his eyes I've never seen before. I can't look away from him. Fire, passion, rage?

"I don't have feelings for you." I harden my features and turn my gaze to his, ignoring the chaotic thoughts about Nixon racing through my mind. "And you fucking her just solidified that."

He screws his face into a grimace. "I was barely inside her. It doesn't even count."

Bastard.

"I wouldn't want you anyway," he seethes when he realizes I'm not going to give in to him or admit there could be anything between us.

He leans in, his lips spraying spittle over my face as he tries to finish me off. "You're damaged goods."

Alcohol comes off him in waves, and I flinch from his cruel words, but within seconds, he is shoved away from me. Nixon rears his arm back and hits him with a closed fist, a sickening thud ringing out as it connects with his jaw and sends him to the floor in a heap. Shock washes over Hayden's face, igniting his eyes and widening them. He starts to get up, but he's wobbly, totally taken off guard by his younger brother.

"You fucking little bastard!" he roars, but Nixon kicks out with his foot, landing a blow to Hayden's chin, making his head crash back and rebound off the tile floor with a clunk, stealing his consciousness, knocking him out cold.

"Sleep it off," Nixon tells him, his tone so calm, it's like he just laid him on a couch with a blanket and a night nurse.

He turns to me, the towel almost slipping from his narrow hips. They've all been in the pool.

"He's been in the sun too long and had too much to drink. Ignore what he said."

My mouth hangs open, and my tongue struggles to form words. There's no saliva left. I need a drink.

"Is he going to be okay?" I breathe eventually, pointing down at his brother where he lays out cold.

"Do you care?" he scoffs, walking away toward the kitchen.

Dammit.

Just as we come into the kitchen, the front door opens, and Cam comes barrelling through it like a tornado, followed by a stressed looking Trevor.

"Cam!" he shouts after him, who tosses his backpack on the floor and takes the stairs two at a time without looking back or replying.

Shaking his head, and placing his hands on his hips, Trevor exhales a defeated breath.

"What's going on?" Nix demands. Trevor raises his brow, giving Nix's apparel a once over.

"Should I be asking you that question?"

"Trev?" Nix ignores his assumptions.

"The school called me. Cam got into a fight with some other kids."

What? No way. Cam is placid, and a caring kid. He hates violence.

"Cam?" Nix scoffs in disbelief.

Trevor runs a hand through his hair and comes to

take a seat at the breakfast bar. I pull out a bottle of water for myself and a first aid kit. We can't leave Hayden like that, no matter how much he deserved a right hook.

"Yes, those were my thoughts. Some jocks cornered him over a girl, if you can believe that. I thought Cam might have been into boys until this happened," Trevor declares, almost making me spit out my water.

Nixon's fist clenches and eyes narrow as the atmosphere thickens once again.

"Why the fuck would you say that?" The tone in his voice is deadly, making my skin heat.

Trevor holds his hands up in defence. "Calm down. I didn't know you were a homophobe. Shit."

"I don't give a shit if people are gay, but insinuating Cam is just because he's not dipping his dick in every female with a pulse is insulting to him and gay men."

"How the hell are you seventeen?" Trevor shakes his head in disbelief.

"How the hell are you fifty with those shoes?" Nixon

counters.

Trevor gets to his feet, his eyes twitching. "I'm not fifty, you little shit."

"Whatever you say, Grandpa."

Shaking his head, Trevor mutters, "I take it back, you are definitely seventeen."

Just as he finishes his sentence, a drowsy looking Hayden joins us, holding one hand to his head and the other around his stomach like he's about to vomit. I move away from everyone, not sure what's about to go down.

"What the hell happened to you?" Trevor asks, studying him. There's blood on his lips and a bruise already blossoming on his cheek.

"Nothing." Hayden glowers over at Nixon.

The beat of my own heart pounds in my ears as my nerves fray.

"Well, you look like shit, and the school couldn't get ahold of you today," Trevor informs him. "You begged to be his guardian. Jumped through all the goddamn hoops. And when it mattered, you weren't there." When Hayden doesn't reply, Trevor carries on. "You weren't at the office today, why?"

He's completely ignoring the fact that Hayden has clearly taken a beating.

"I had other things to do."

Trevor gestures toward the front door. "Does this thing have anything to do with the redhead I saw storming out of here like her ass was on fire?"

Nixon snorts. "It's not her ass that will be on fire if he keeps fucking everything that flashes their gash to him."

Gash? Nice.

"Gross, Nix," I reprimand.

"Yeah, gash? Seriously?" Hayden twists up his lip.

"Okay, I'm going," Trevor announces, shaking his head. "Try not to kill each other, and make sure Rowan eats."

"I'm right here," I reveal, but he waves me off with a, "Yeah, yeah."

Once he's gone, Hayden points a finger to Nixon, who just offers him a smirk in return.

"You ever try that shit again, and I won't be responsible for what I do," he warns him.

"Not responsible for what? Going lights out like a bitch," Nixon torments.

"You caught me off guard," Hayden growls.

"Let's go again then." Nix squares his shoulders.

"Guys," I bark, having enough of the testosterone for one day. Neither looks my way; they're too busy staring each other out.

"If you're going to act like uneducated morons, can you do it outside?" I open the fridge and pull out some fresh chicken.

"What's she doing?" I hear Hayden ask.

"I have no clue, but I hope it's not cooking because she sucks," Nixon replies.

"I'm right here, guys." I roll my eyes and push the chicken across the counter.

Nix's brow quirks up, and I smile my sweetest grin.

"Momma wants chicken."

EIGHT

N I X O N

#7 Trait of a Psychopath

Narcissism

CAM DIDN'T COME DOWN FOR DINNER. THAT BOY loves his food. I knock on his door and push it open when he doesn't answer.

Looking around his room and finding nothing, I frown. Where the hell is he?

I go to my room and place the plate of food I brought up for him on the dresser. It's then I see the bulge in my covers and hear his soft snores. My back straightens and fist clenches. He only ever does this when he's upset. I should have come up and checked on him when Trevor left, but I got distracted with Rowan.

Taking a seat on the edge of my bed, I nudge his shoulder. When he moves to face me, he's groggy and there's a purple bruise forming under his eye. "What the fuck happened?" I demand wanting his version of events not the watered down shit Trevor gave me.

He won't look at me, and I hate it. I left school early today because I hate trig and couldn't wait to get home to Ro. She wasn't here, and instead, I had to watch Hayden make a fool out of himself and Suzanne.

I don't agree with Rowan blaming him for her being willing to fuck him. It takes two and all that fucking jazz, but he was only using her to make a point—a shitty one that made my blood boil. It failed him, though. And for the first time since Eric died, I saw life in Rowan's eyes. Not for Hayden—no, she was looking at me. A hum vibrates in my chest every time I think about the longing in her eyes. It was pure fucking longing.

Cam shifting under the cover draws my attention back to him.

"Cam, talk to me, bro."

He shuffles around and sits up, resting his elbows on his knees. "Is that food?" He nods his head toward the dresser. I grin and jump up to get it for him.

"Here. Now, talk."

"Masters and Grayson got fist happy because Grayson's girlfriend dumped him and has been following me around like a lost puppy all day."

He lifts his shoulders and runs a hand through his untamed mane. Kid is a classic chick magnet. There is no working for it or pursuing girls. Cam just has a way about him that attracts most women. Doesn't matter their age, occupation, intelligence—they all turn to putty when he flashes his smile their way. Boys like Grayson should know better than to fuck with my brother, but it seems a lesson is needed.

My muscles coil and red-hot anger seeps into my pores, saturating my insides.

"Did you hit them back?" I try to keep my voice

calm, but I'm angry. Real fucking angry. I want to break things—mainly their faces.

"I'm the brains in the family, not the brawn." He grins at me, and I relax a little. I rub a hand over his hair to ruffle it, and he bats me away and shovels food into his mouth.

I've always given Cam a side of me no one else sees. Rowan is the same. She gets a part of me just for her, because they're the only two people I haven't visualized killing before. They need me, and I need them. It's a sobering thought to actually admit to myself that I give a shit and need people.

"Don't worry about those assholes. I'll sort this out." I stand and go toward the shower room.

"I'll deal with this myself, Nix," Cam calls after me. It's muffled from the food he's shoveling in his gob. I pause to let him finish. "I may not like using my fists, but I have my ways." He winks, and I laugh. The little fucker is right. He is the brains of the family.

"Did you say something?"

I look down at a brunette who's staring up at me. Is she talking to me?

"You were mumbling to yourself," she announces.

She stares wide-eyed up at me, like she's trying to figure me out. Good luck with that.

Slamming my locker door shut, I shift past her, but she grabs my arm.

I don't recoil, but it does make me want to shove her to the floor. I hate people touching me. People who aren't *my* people. People who aren't *her*.

Fuck. I hate how fuzzy the lines are becoming with Rowan. We need to just admit the inevitable. She's mine and I'm hers. End of. It's how it was always meant to be.

Every instinct I have tells me we're supposed to be together, but it's such a complicated fucking mess, it's murkier than my already overcast thoughts.

My brothers may not be open to the idea, and if there's one thing I know about Rowan, it's that she gives a shit what they think. Even Hayden. She blames herself for what her father did and tiptoes around the place like she's frightened we're all going to wake up one day and come to that conclusion. She has no idea how much she's loved by all of us. Their feelings may not be as intense and powerful as mine, but they all love her. We grew up together. And what we've been through together forms a bond bigger than anything else.

"Did you hear me?" the girl asks. Shit, she said something?

"No," I growl, snatching my arm from her grip.

She bites her lip and shyly looks around me. "I was wondering...the dance is coming up and..."

"I don't do dances." Fuck, how many of these things do they have a year?

"Oh no," she says with a laugh, shaking her head like I just told a joke.

"Everyone knows you don't do dances or anything school related, including high school girls."

Oh, is that the rumor roaming these halls?

"So, what the fuck you asking for?" I yawn. Damn, I'm bored with this shit. Is it time to go home yet?

I rub a hand across the back of my neck, giving it a squeeze. Why the fuck am I still standing here? *Because she's blocking my escape.*

"I was wondering if your brother Camden had asked anyone yet." Her eyes dart around me again, and curiosity nags at me. I turn to see my brother a few feet down the corridor chatting with some girls, a blonde one especially hanging on his every word. Cam got double dosed in the looks department. That kid got all the best features from both parents, and women, young and old, trip over their jaws wherever the fucker goes. He's never really shown much interest in girls—too much going on in his head. The kid is stupid clever—numbers, computers, anything. He's going through a phase where he's into watching the news, and I'm just waiting on him to announce he's going to be president one day. I wouldn't put it past him.

"Do I look like his keeper?" I growl down at girl who has robbed me of too much time. I was his keeper, until recently, when Rowan consumed my every fucking waking thought and ounce of spare time. I should make more of an effort to keep an eye on him.

"Well..." She looks a little embarrassed and digs around in her purse. I can't believe I'm still standing here entertaining this shit. I'm going soft.

"Here." She hands me a card—a fucking card with her number and social media info.

This is fucking high school, and she's handing me business type card with her social media info. Damn, I hate that I was born into the twenty-first century.

I move past her and chuck her card in the first trashcan I pass.

Pushing the door to the boys changing room, I nod my head to a couple of the guys who play basketball with me. They grin and go stand by the door to keep a look out.

I'm not one for following rules, but I haven't spent years in this shithole to lose my chance at graduating in the final hour.

Grayson is sitting on a bench bending down to tie his laces. Perfect position, asshole.

I rear my foot back and kick it forward, colliding with his chin. His teeth clank together so loud, a boy behind him cringes and jumps back as Grayson's head moves back with such force, he falls from the bench.

Blood from his mouth creates artwork up the locker.

Masters backs up and tries to flee, but he's pushed forward by some of the guys who know better than to let him past them.

He swings at me, and I grin. Balls of fucking steel. Dodging his hit I land a punch to his jaw. Wrapping his arm under my armpit to keep him from falling over too soon I land a couple more jabs. Making sure to get that eye so it gets a nice shine to it. Grabbing a handful of his hair I smack his head into the locker a couple times before letting him fall to the floor.

He's out cold. I point my finger to Grayson, whose whimpering and covering his fucked up jaw. "Which one of you blackened Cam's eye?" I growl. The pussy points to his unconscious friend.

Bending down I grab the dead weights wrist and drag him to the locker in front of Grayson. Opening the locker door I gesture for Grayson to take Master's hand. He does with trembling limbs. "Hold it right there." I tell him and then slam the door closed over and over until his hand resembles a piece of meat put through a meat grinder.

"Fuck," Grayson mutters through chipped teeth.

"Tell your cunt friend either one of you even look in my brother's direction again, I'll cut your eyes from your head."

If they're brave enough they'll get me expelled but all it will take is a donation to the school to get my slate wiped clean. Swiping the blood spatter from my knuckles

I grin. Worth every fucking penny.

———

Hayden is trying to rub Rowan the wrong way. He's been parading women around the house like they're paid whores. And they might be for all we know.

Their antics echo through the house tonight where I planned a movie night with Ro. She's been so tired lately and doesn't like to go out much. She's convinced people are talking about her, and they probably are, but who gives a fuck? I'd wipe the world clean of all its inhabitants if it pleased her, but her soul is already too heavy. She blames herself for not seeing what her father was. If she knew I did see it inside him, the pain I'd see in her eyes would kill me.

A giggle erupts from outside the room, and every time Rowan hears them, she flinches. I hate that she used to have a thing for Hayden. He's just like Eric and not worthy of her infatuation.

Her stomach moves, and she gasps, rubbing a hand

against her ribs. There's not much room there anymore, and she's uncomfortable most of the time. She waddles rather than walks, and I hear her get up to piss all through the night. She's like a water fountain that won't turn off. A gory scene happens on the screen, but the movie has been shit and doesn't hold either of our attention.

"She's active tonight. Was the Mexican too spicy?" I ask. I made it mild because spices give her heartburn, despite her loving them at the moment.

"No, it was amazing. She's just uncomfortable I think. I know how she feels."

She groans out, lifting her top to rub her bare stomach. It ripples like an alien is about to burst through her flesh.

I reach over and place my hand on top of hers, and she smiles, moving her hand to rest on mine and placing it where the baby kicks my palm. It's pretty incredible to think of a human growing inside her. "Do you want to talk about this?" she asks, brushing the tips of her fingers over my bruised knuckles.

"Just taking care of what's mine." Her brow pinches but she nods her head and sighs.

"Have you thought about a name for her yet?" I ask changing the subject.

She groans. "No."

Giggles screech closer to our space, and then a blonde bitch comes barrelling into the room in panties and an open shirt like she fucking owns the place.

Her bra is on display, and she's covered in little bruises made from someone sucking on her skin. She skids to a stop when she sees us, and her eyes widen.

"Nix," the girl coos my name like a caress, like it's personal and she's knows parts of me she doesn't. It's then I realize it's the girl from school who was all over Cam in the corridor. Just as I think of him, he appears.

Shirtless and his hair in disarray.

"Sorry." He grins. "She escaped the dungeon."

A gasp leaves Rowan at his comment. Cam has been

using the basement as his own space, and Hayden keeps making jokes about him keeping women down there. It's a little too close to home for Rowan, and Cam can be a little odd, but harmful he isn't.

He's just clever—too fucking clever—and that makes him appear different to people like Hayden, who are what you see. Eric two-point-oh.

"I'm Amanda." The blonde wiggles her fingers at us like we give a shit what her name is.

"I know who you are." Rowan rolls her eyes.

"Oh, I forgot you knew Grayson." The blonde nods.

"Grayson?" I ask, nonchalant, but feeling anything but.

"Yeah, I used to tutor him," Rowan informs me. "Amanda's his girlfriend."

"Was." Cam grins, and I smirk. Fucking A. So, he really did have a plan to get back at the douche.

Amanda giggles and bites her lip.

"Sorry to interrupt your movie." Cam grabs

Amanda's arm and tugs her in the direction of the door.

"That's a new side to Cam." Rowan nudges me with her knee.

"I'm not going to gossip with you, woman," I snort.

"Boring." She pulls her top down over her stomach and plonks her foot in my lap.

"At least rub a girl's swollen feet if you're not going to gossip."

NINE

N I X O N

#8 Trait of a Psychopath

Blameless

HAYDEN IS SUITED AND BOOTED WHEN I COME DOWN to make breakfast. He's reading a newspaper and swigging from a coffee mug. It's freaky as hell.

"Hey." I announce my arrival, and he eyes me over his cup.

"Morning."

I check my watch—an expensive and over the top watch Camden bought for me at Christmas—and look over at him as I pull out a skillet to fry some bacon.

"You got time for breakfast?"

He holds his mug up and quirks a brow.

"Bad habit to start, brother."

"I'll get something at the office."

At the office. Damn, he sounds like Eric. It's crazy how adjusted he's become to the role. I always thought he would be the wild card—ride away from us all on a Harley with a fuck you thrown over his shoulder—but here he is, taking the bull by the horns. He has days when he slips back into the Hayden we all grew up with, the Hayden who fucks little redheads to hurt their best friends, but he's entitled to slips.

It's because of him Cam and I get to stay here. He knows when he's being a dick and accepts when one of us needs to put him in his place.

"You seen Brock?" he asks me, putting down his paper.

"He's like passing ships since Eri—Dad died. We should start paying Ethan rent and board for him."

I crack some eggs into a bowl and whisk them.

Hayden rubs a hand over his neck and sighs. "Maybe

we should try a family dinner?"

I stop stirring and stare at him. "What's that?"

Pointing his finger and walking backwards, he says, "I'll bring the food, you get Brock and Cam at the table." He picks up his jacket and heads for the door.

"And Rowan," I shout.

He takes a few steps back so he can see me again around the protruding wall separating the kitchen from the living area.

"Maybe just Pearsons tonight."

Fuck that. She's carrying a Pearson.

"Don't fucking evil glare me, Nix. I need to talk to you three about the will without her there."

"Why?"

"Because she's not in it."

"So, she won't care."

"That's not the point, just don't give me a hard time for once. Please."

Narrowing my eyes, I nod once.

Brown wallpaper, green and blue furniture...I hope Dr. Winters didn't pay a designer for this look.

"You appear agitated today."

Oh, do I, Doc? Fuck, I'll be glad when I don't have to come here. I don't like being under the control of anyone, and with Eric gone, I have rules I need to play by to make sure I get to stay put. Eighteen can't come quick enough. The best part about that magic number is getting my inheritance. Trevor and Levi tried to have a say in when we would all get our dad's money, but it wasn't up to them. Good old Eric had a will. Our trust funds are nothing compared to the inheritance money we'll each receive when we each hit that magic age. Hayden got Eric's shares in the company with Eric's wishes for Brock to later become a part of the empire, whereas Cam and I got properties and just money—more money than we could ever need.

Eric knew I had no interest in ever becoming part of Four Fathers Freight. And Cam was going to rule the fucking world one day. He would never be happy sitting behind a desk doing something that didn't have purpose. Cam wants to leave an impact.

I half expected to find a note in his will announcing him not being my real father and cutting me out. It's weird always feeling like you don't belong to someone while living in their denial with them.

If Eric did ever question my blood matching his, he didn't stop him naming me as his and giving me the same amount of assets as each of my brothers.

Eric didn't make changes to the will in the last year, so Rowan wasn't on it. She'll never have to worry about money, however. She has her own trust fund. And if the house ever gets sorted next door, that should belong to her as well.

She hasn't once ventured over there, though. It's a tomb.

I'll never let her worry about anything ever again.

"Tell me about Rowan," Winters says, like she can

read my mind.

"What about her?"

"Tell me anything."

"Her ankles swell up lately." I shrug. There, that's something.

A genuine smile tilts her lips. "That's common in pregnancy."

"Is it?" I ask, but I know this. I know everything about pregnancy because I can read and read every book there is.

"Are you looking forward to the new arrival?"

I relax back into the suffocating couch I hate.

"Rowan will be a good mom."

"I'm sure she will," she agrees. "And you and your brothers are all close. Will that be the same with the new arrival?"

"This is different."

Fuck, I wish I could stuff that back in my mouth. Her pupils dilate and she shifts her pen over her paper briefly.

"Why is it different?"

She's such a cunt. Like she doesn't know why it's different.

"Age gap."

I smile. And she squints.

"How are the dynamics in the house with Rowan there?"

Nice try.

"Feels the same as it always has. In one way or another, Rowan has always been there."

"What about when you bring girlfriends over to the house? Does this cause any problems for Rowan?"

What the fuck kind of question is that?

"Maybe you should ask her?"

"Tell me how you see Rowan—as a sister, a friend?"

"I don't want to talk about her anymore."

"What do you want to talk about?"

"Nothing."

"That would be a waste of our sessions."

"I think Camden has a girlfriend."

Her perfectly shaped brow peaks at this information. Camden comes here too. Maybe he hasn't mentioned this to her.

Sike, bitch.

"What about you?"

"What about me?"

"Do you have a girlfriend?"

Girlfriends are a chore—one I don't have time for. The only girl I ever let me talk into being her boyfriend betrayed me and made me almost lose my grip on reality.

Nixon nine months ago

The world has always been a question mark to me. I've never understood where my place in it is. The only people I give two shits about are my baby brother and her, Rowan, my best friend and the girl I just saw kissing Eric.

Nausea was my first response, followed by undiluted

hate for Eric.

He's fucking old and disgusting. Rowan just turned eighteen—eighteen. She may be legal, but he's a fucking pervert. End of.

Plan...I need a plan. This can't be happening.

"Nix, here are the notes you asked for." A girl from my English class hands me her booklet and coyly smiles up at me. The skirt she's wearing shows more thigh than suitable for high school, and her tits are pushed up so far by a bra too small, they're creating a four tit impression through her shirt. When I don't speak, she talks again.

"So, I was wondering if you wanted to hang or something tonight?"

Images of Rowan flash through my mind, and I think maybe two can play that game. Maybe if I try getting with someone else, I can forget about her and let it go—let her go. Fuck that. I'm used to winning what I want, and this...
"What's your name?"

"Roxy," she states, like I should already know that.

Well, Roxy, you're going to be a distraction while I let this stupid infatuation Rowan has for Eric runs its course.

———

I hate bringing Roxy back here, but I need the distraction from Rowan running around the place shacked up with fucking Eric. Images taunt me—of what he's touching, kissing...

"I'll suck you off."

I blink and look up at Roxy, who's straddling me on my bed. I'm trying to read a stupid chem book for a test tomorrow, but she's needy as hell. Wiggling her ass, she groans from the friction she's creating. Her hands lean down onto my hips, and her eyes widen. "Is that something in your pocket, or are you just glad to see me?"

It's actually my new flip knife I bought off the internet. It arrived today, and I haven't had time to play with it. I told myself I was buying it for a camping trip, but truth is, it just fascinated me.

"Go get us some drinks." *I slap her ass, and she*

giggles. It's fake as fuck and makes me want to gag her so she can't speak, laugh, breathe...

"Okay," she sighs, slipping off me.

Watching her leave, I debate getting up and locking the door so she can't come back in, but I'll just settle for getting a drink and sending her on her merry way for the night.

Girls are horny. People always assume boys are, and in fairness we are, but fuck, Roxy is like a nympho at times. It's hard work faking attraction for someone all the fucking time.

I can hear her outside my room talking to Hayden, then their voices fade and a door closes. Motherfucker.

I don't particularly want her, but she's my distraction—not his. No one makes a fool of me. Sitting up, my chem book clatters to the floor as I swing my legs off the bed and get up.

Brock almost collides with me as he exits his room at the same time.

"What's up your ass?" he asks, but I don't stop to chat. I boot open Hayden's door to find him and Roxy fooling around on his bed. Hayden, the prick, doesn't even get up. Roxy screeches and giggles like she's not in here cheating, and these bitches wonder why I don't date high school chicks.

"You've been a bad girl," I tease her, and she grabs her shirt and runs past me out the room and down the stairs.

"Thanks for the loan, bro." Hayden smirks. I give him the middle finger and give chase to Roxy.

We hit the foyer, and she throws her shirt at me, swaying on her feet.

I chuck it to the floor and shake my head at her.

"You can't have us all."

"I only want you," she coos, making me want to slap the shit out of her.

Her nipples harden and peak through the lace of her bra. She slips her shorts down her legs and kicks them over to me.

"Run," I warn, and jolt forward.

She takes off out the front door and across the drive onto Rowan's property.

Excited chortles ring from her as she tries to out run me. It's a pathetic attempt on her part. She's desperate to be caught. I wrap an arm around her and lift her feet from the ground, swinging her around and covering her fat mouth with the palm of my hand.

She wriggles her ass on me, and I release her. I half expect her to run again, but she doesn't. "You want to suck my brother's dick instead of mine?" I admonish her.

Shaking her head, she hums, "No."

Pushing down on her shoulder, I guide her to her knees. Her small hands come up to untie my shorts, and my hand goes to the knife in my pocket.

I pull it free and imagine holding it to her neck, letting the blade cut in enough to stop her from talking— enough to make her cry and question whether she's going to die.

"Nixon," Jaxson Wheeler barks, stepping onto his

porch.

Nice timing, old man. Roxy gasps and screams, jumping up and running back to my house. I grin over at him.

"What do you think you're doing?" he asks, but there's an understanding in his eyes. Like he knew my thoughts in that moment. I take off after Roxy, ignoring his question.

Roxy is standing frozen in the foyer when I come into the house. Hayden is standing opposite her, wearing just a towel.

"I was just asking your friend if she wanted to have a late-night swim. Pick up where we left off."

Hayden winks at her, and she turns an extra dark shade of red.

She looks over at me and folds her arms over her tits like she's now a prude.

I nod my head at my brother. "She loves getting wet. Have at it." And with that, I saunter past them into the kitchen to get my own drink.

"Nix?" Roxy calls out to me, but I ignore her. I'm done with her. Trying to use her as a distraction is pointless. She only makes me want to kill things. Mainly her.

Present

"Where do you go when you zone out like that?"

I shrug my shoulders. "Just thinking about the question."

"I think you're reliving moments in your head and I wish you would share them with me instead."

"I don't like having girlfriends. I pretended Rowan was my girlfriend once."

One of her brows dip.

"Why?"

"Because her dad was suspicious of the time she was spending over at our house."

"So, you protected their relationship?"

I cringe at the way she says it.

It wasn't to protect Eric from being a pervert; it was to stop her from getting in trouble with her father. He would have stopped her leaving his house if he knew she was seeing Eric. He could have packed her up and moved away from him—*from me*. I couldn't allow him time to plan. We needed more time. It had to be in the moment of discovery so he reacted in the moment, ending Eric, not taking my Rowan away from me.

"I've always wanted to protect her."

I knew losing Eric would hurt her. She was infatuated, and it's normal for girls to go through that, but she's getting over it now, and we're all better off without Eric around.

TEN

N I X O N

#9 Trait of a Psychopath

Impulsive

BREATHE IN AND OUT. *IN AND OUT,* I REPLAY OVER and over in my mind as I sit in the tub. I stretch my arm out to try to snag my cell again from the counter, but it's just out of reach. I mumble through the pain as my stomach contracts again.

Damn it, I should have waited until one of the boys were home before getting in the tub.

My legs wobble as I try to stand. They feel like jelly. Pain burns in my hip, and everything feels too tight.

"Fucccck," I groan out, then hear the front door slam closed. It echoes through the entire house, and relief floods me.

"Hey, who's there?" I call. "Someone, hello!" I call again.

Footfalls sound on the stairs, and I sag back. "Ro?"

Nixon. Thank God. "Yes, in here," I call out. I left the bedroom door open, thankfully, and this entire place is made of tiled and wooden floors, so sound carries.

The handle on the door drops, but I had locked the bathroom door. Fuck.

"Rowan?" he mumbles through the wood separating us.

"I'm in labor," I cry out. Cusses ring out from behind the door, and then a thud sounds and wood splinters as Nixon comes through the door, tearing it off its hinges.

A yelp escapes me, and I wrap a hand over my breasts to cover them.

"Why the hell would you take a bath when no one is here?" He looks pissed, but I don't have time to worry about his overprotectiveness.

"Shut up and help me," I groan. Grabbing a towel, he takes my arm to help me to stand. "I can't stand up. My legs keep giving out," I sob.

"That's okay. Shhh, don't worry."

But I am, I'm not ready to be a mom. This wasn't supposed to be like this. Everything hits me at once. Tears pour down my cheeks, and my heart concaves.

"It's okay, Rowan. I promise." Nixon tries to calm me as he leans down and scoops me up. I don't fight him. Even though I'm butt ass naked and the water from my now lukewarm bath drenches his clothes.

He moves with ease with me in his hold, taking me to my room and placing me on the bed. I take the towel he put over his shoulder and cover my body as he goes to rummage through my dresser for some clothes.

"Did you make your maternity bag for the hospital?"

He's focused and dressing me like I'm a child. Socks, sweats, no panties, followed by a sweater over my head and him lifting each of my arms through the armholes.

"Thanks, Nix. For being here," I hiccup on a sob.

———

Nothing about labor felt natural. *It's the most natural thing in the world*, the nurses kept telling me while a human tried to tear her way into the world.

But my body just refused to do its job, so my healthy Erica was delivered in a surgical room. "Already a drama queen," Nixon had joked, but the fear in his features and dilated pupils gave him away.

He was scared for me—for us.

"How are you feeling?" a nurse asks me while she fiddles with the IV pumping fluids into me.

That's a loaded question. I offer her a smile, and she pats my arm and leaves us alone once again.

How am I feeling? I want to be numb. I wish I could stay numb.

Pain, sharp and constant, annoys me from my hip. I've just had a baby cut from my womb not four hours ago, yet it's the stupid hip that's giving me problems.

This day should be so different, but here I am, a single mother with no real family.

Eric's sons have taken care of me, but it doesn't end the weird hollow hole I feel inside me since losing their father...and mine.

I still want to hate my dad for what he did, and I do, but it doesn't erase the love I still feel for him. It's such a weird thing to feel: hate and love in equal measure.

I look at my cell phone and frown. Still nothing from Lucy. She promised she'd be here for the birth of my baby girl, but she didn't make it, and she hasn't visited since. I text Trevor to ask if he's heard from her, but ten minutes pass, and he still doesn't reply.

The room door barges open, startling me, and Nixon fills the space. He'd gone on a caffeine run. He looks uninhabited, his eyes wide and jaw tense.

I sit up, nerves eating away at my stomach. "What is it?" I ask, breathless.

"Lucy. Trevor found her drugged and naked at her

house."

The room expands, then closes in around me. "What?"

"She's here in the hospital. They're trying to determine what's in her system, but she's still alive."

Camden and Brock push into the room past Nixon. They look pale and shaken.

"She'll be okay," I comfort them, but really, it's to comfort myself. We can't lose anyone else. I can't. What the hell happened?

"Ro, that's not all," Nixon says in a tone I've never heard him use before. It's almost fear. Camden moves to the bed, and takes my hand, squeezing it.

"What? What is it?" I plead, terror beginning to eat its way up my throat.

"The baby. She's gone."

"The baby. She's gone."

"The baby. She's gone."

The words roll around my mind like a carousel. My

body moves to stand, but my legs aren't working. I fumble and drop to the floor. All three of the boys surround me, but I can't focus.

"Where's my baby!" I shout.

I think of her steely blue eyes identical to her father's, and a sob clogs my throat.

"Rowan, we'll get her back," Brock vows, staring so intently at me, I swear it's Eric incarnate.

"Where's my baby!" I screech.

"We think your father has taken her," Nixon states.

What? No. No.

I'm losing my touch on reality. Darkness clouds around me, and I drown in the ache—the pain of knowing he's taken her to punish me.

To start over.

To have someone who loves him.

She's gone.

She's gone.

She's gone...

ELEVEN ———

N I X O N

#10 Trait of a Psychopath

Cruelty to animals

DA DUM. DA DUM. DA DUM. DA DUM.

My heartbeat pounds in my head as I pace the bed they've had to sedate Rowan in. I think she finally broke. This pushed her over the edge.

I place a kiss to her forehead and meet my brothers in the corridor.

"Police are checking the security footage now," Hayden informs me. His hair is all over the place from him running his hands through it.

"Lucy's in a bad way." Cam hugs his arms around himself. He's rocking in a chair, looking fragile as shit.

"It's all going to be okay," I reassure them.

"How the fuck do you know that?" Brock demands.

I can't tell them that, so I just shake my head.

"Because it has to be," I offer instead, before closing the space between Hayden and me. "I need you to be in there with her, and don't leave her until I'm back."

"Where are you going?" he asks.

"Hay." I place hand on his chest and look him direct in the eye. "Please just stay with her and don't leave that room—not even to piss."

His eyes bore into mine studying, searching for answers to a million questions firing off in his mind.

"Trust me," I urge him.

"I'm coming with you." Cam stands up.

"No." I shake my head and go over to him. "I need you here in case they find Erica. She's going to need to be with family, and Rowan could be out for hours."

He nods his head in understanding.

"Trevor's in pieces over Lucy," Brock chokes out.

Ethan, his best friend, grips his shoulder to offer his support, and says, "We'll stay for Rowan, for Lucy, for all of them."

I nod in agreement.

"I'll be back soon."

I leave them to take care of my girl and check my cell phone again to re-read the message Jaxson sent me.

Home sweet home.

━━━━

There's an undercover cop car parked a couple feet from his old house. Pulling my car into our drive, I check the yard, my guard up. This could be a trap. Perhaps he's changed his mind on the not killing me shit. He can try.

I let myself into our house and go straight to Eric's office and crack his safe.

Taking out the Glock and checking it's loaded, I stuff it into the back of my jeans and slip out the back door.

The moon lights the darkened sky, giving me a clear view of the door I once built into the fence to go between our house and Rowan's. It's open.

He knows I'm coming, so trying to be sneaky is useless. I make my way over there. The grass is overgrown and the place looks rundown after standing empty for months.

We should do it up and put it on the market, or bulldoze it so Rowan doesn't have to see it anymore.

Drapes blow through the open doors in the back of the house, and I listen for a baby's cries, but it's eerie fucking silent.

I don't know how I know, but I just fucking know he hasn't hurt her.

She looks too much like her mother. And baby killing isn't his style.

The place smells like it always has as I enter. I thought it might be musty, but it smells clean, and like sandalwood.

Looking around the downstairs, I don't see any movement.

Just as my foot hits the bottom stair, a sliver of light

comes from the basement door.

That's creepy, an icy chill races up my spine but adrenaline is pumping hard through my bloodstream to counter act it. Police went through this place with a fine tooth comb after they uncovered my mother's body, but nothing was found as far as I know.

Still, basements are creepy when you know a murderer is down there. I always thought I had those traits inside me—the urge—but things have changed for me since Eric's been gone—since learning what really happened to our mother—since getting Rowan back. There's this anger inside me but it's more a defense, to protect the people I care about. That's makes me normal, right? It has to.

Pushing open the door, I take the stairs down, and my heartrate speeds up when Jaxson comes into sight, Erica cradled in his arms.

"This is where your mother tried to whore herself out," he announces before my feet even hit the bottom step.

"I'm not here to talk about what a slut my mother was. I already know." I smirk, my eyes examining the baby without giving away that I'm doing just that.

He grins back at me with teeth on show. "Is she the reason you are what you are?" he asks, moving around the table positioned in the center of the space.

"Can it be that simple?" I counter.

The baby makes a soft murmur, and Jaxson rocks her in his arms, with care and experience.

"I remember Rowan like this. Innocent. Unspoiled by the world," he reminisces.

My cell rings, snapping him from the moment. He looks to my jean pocket and raises a brow. "You want to get that?"

His face is so stoic, it almost makes me laugh.

"It's probably just Brock updating me on Lucy."

Brown irises expand, almost disappearing, giving way to the blacks of his pupils.

He must remember Lucy. "Where is she?"

"Who?"

"Lucy." There's an urgency to his tone that makes my stomach knot.

"Was it you who did that to her?" I ask in disbelief.

"Where is she?" he demands again, and his tone is deadly. Usually, I'd taunt him, but his demeanor gives no room for messing around and Erica is still in his grip.

"Hospital. She's dying, and they don't know what she's taken, or been given."

I take a step toward him, and he doesn't move. He's very comfortable and confident being here, even as a wanted fugitive.

"Police are outside," I inform him, and he rolls his eyes.

"They're pathetic. I came in through your house. I always hated that gateway you created, but seems to have proven useful in this case."

"What do you know about Lucy?" I prod, and he

sighs.

"Lucy, Lucy, Lucy. I see the police have been down here." He changes the subject.

"They found bodies in your backyard." I shrug like it's fair for them to have searched the place.

He scoffs, making Erika jolt in his grasp.

"They didn't find shit. I gave you the bodies."

"Thanks," I deadpan, and he grins over at me.

"I always liked you, Nixon."

"Is that a compliment?" I move forward a couple more inches, my hand reaching around and taking the gun from the back of my jeans.

His eyes drop to my weapon, but he ignores it, like I'm holding air.

Lifting his free hand, he raps his knuckles on the wall.

Tap, tap.

Tap, tap.

A crease forms on his forehead, and then the brick pops out from the wall.

Well, shit.

He pulls out a handful of pictures and tosses them on to the table.

"Lucy is part of my collection," he announces.

What the fuck?

Da dum, da dum, da dum.

My jaw unhinges as I step forward and brush my hand through the photographs, spreading them out over the space.

Blonde, brunette, tan, creamy flesh, hundreds of photos of different women.

My hand stops on one of Lucy, and I look up at him.

"Are these women dead?"

"I've been in your house, seen where Rowan sleeps, the nursery you have set up for the baby."

"She belongs with us, and I think you know that," I state, waggling the photo in my hand.

"This...this will kill Rowan." I shake my head, looking back down at the dozens of women. "When she sees these..." I frown, thinking about the way she blames herself over Eric and how it tortures her to think of Jaxson as a monster. This will fucking kill her.

"Do you think I'm like you?" I ask suddenly. All my thoughts of us being alike slam into me. Will I become like him? Kill women for...what? Kicks? Sense of power?

"What is it you're really asking?"

"Do you think I'm a psychopath?" I ask bluntly.

He laughs and moves his hand to the baby's neck.

"If I were to kill someone you love, would you care?" His eyes bore into mine, flaying me right down to the core.

Would I care? Fuck yes.

"If you're searching the sea of people you love in your mind right now, then you're probably not a psychopath." He narrows his stare on me.

"Give me the baby and I'll let you leave here," I offer, and his lips twist into a simper.

"Or you can put the gun down and I'll let you leave

here," he counters.

"Not going to happen. Why the hell did you want me here?"

"I want to return a daughter to her father."

Da dum. Da dum. Da dum.

"What the fuck does that mean?" I growl, picturing Eric's dead eyes staring up from the hole in the backyard. As if reading my mind, Jaxson tuts.

"Not that cunt. You—her real father."

Da dum. Da dum. Da dum.

"Girls need their fathers, and she's going to need a daddy. You'll take care of both of them. I know you will."

I nod my head in confirmation. Yes I will, until my dying breath.

"Why did you take her then?" I query.

"To spend some time with her. I couldn't risk staying at the hospital. I'm a wanted man." He smiles, like he's happy about that fact.

He gestures with a head nod to the gun I'm holding

and the table.

"Put the weapon on the table and push it over to me."

Silence. Fuck, I don't want to give him the gun.

"You can't hold that and the baby, Nixon. Make a choice." The smiles are gone, agitation replacing the happy, not-give-a-shit vibe from seconds before.

Placing the gun on the table, I push it to the other side.

He picks it up and walks over to me, handing over Erica. Relief at feeling her weight in my grip makes my eyes close briefly.

Taking her in my arms, her soft, small body cocoons against my chest.

A calm washes over me, and I feel like I can take a breath for the first time since finding Rowan in labor.

He waves the gun at me to get my attention, and instinctively, my hands tighten on the baby as I turn my back to him.

"Don't let Rowan find these." He talks about the

pictures, but I already plan on burning them in the pit outback.

"Relax," he tells me cradling his frame over mine and slipping his hand into my pocket taking out my cell phone.

"What are you doing? Calling a cab?" I jest.

"Saving my sweet Lucy," he croons, placing the cell to his ear.

He walks over toward the stairs and begins reeling off medical jargon into the phone as he takes the steps two at a time.

I don't move for a good ten seconds, just clinging to Erica for dear life.

"I've got you, baby girl. I'll never let go. I promise."

━━━━━

Hayden paces the corridor, burning a hole in the floor.

"I couldn't just shoot him, Hay. He was holding the fucking baby."

He swipes a hand through his hair and sits, then stands. "You shouldn't have let him get away."

Yeah, because he would have done shit differently. If Hayden had shown up there, he wouldn't have left. He'd be in the wilderness that yard has become.

"Give him a break," Cam shouts, shocking us all. "Our sister is in there being fed by her mom because of Nixon. Not me, not you or Brock—Nixon got her home." He throws his arms around my shoulders and hugs me. "Thank you for getting her home."

Coughing to announce his presence, Trevor looks like he's been hit by a ten-ton truck and was dragged for eight blocks. There's some chick in the corridor with him, her eyes swollen from tears.

"How is she?" I ask.

"Responding well to the new antibiotics. I need some answers from you." He nods his head as crinkles cut into his eyes. I need answers from him. It's something I've never pursued, because, if I'm honest with myself, I'm terrified of the answer. If we share DNA, why hasn't he wanted us tested—wanted me?

How could he watch his best friend raise a kid who's his? It's not like I was a happy fucking kid. I hated my volatile parents.

"Why did Jaxson Wheeler call me from your cell phone?"

Hayden shuffles past me and goes to stand next to the girl who I don't recognize but he clearly does.

"I have a question for you," I counter, sick of dancing around the question everyone must be thinking.

His frown line pinches and his shoulders tense. "Okay?"

Fuck, I didn't want to do this in front of my brothers, but fuck them. Fuck him.

"Are you my real dad?"

A chorus of, "What the fuck?" comes from my brothers, but not Trevor. He looks pained at the question.

He moves toward me, placing his hands on my

shoulders.

"No, why would you ever think that?"

I scoff. We look the fucking same. He must see that. My brothers must see that. Eric had to have seen that.

"I look like you, and I always knew deep down Eric wasn't my dad."

Hayden pushes Trevor out the way and grasps my face in his palms. "Mom wouldn't cheat. She was always accusing Dad of cheating. You look like Mom's brother and Dad had us tested anyway." Hayden rests his head on mine.

"Mom didn't have a brother," Brock interjects.

Hayden releases me with an exhale. "Yes, she does. He's just a piece of shit she hadn't spoken to since she was a kid, anyway that's not the fucking point. Nix I have the proof you are Eric's."

"How the fuck do you know this shit?" Brock asks the question I want the answer to.

"I found paternity tests for us all in Dad's insurance

policy." He rolls his eyes.

Motherfucker.

"I can't believe you thought I was your dad, Nix. I wish you came to me sooner with this so I could have put your mind at rest. I loved my wife, and your father. I never would have betrayed them that way. Or you."

My legs give out, and I collapse into the seat behind me, dropping my head into my hands.

I honestly didn't expect this outcome. All the years I thought Eric wasn't my dad.

"You okay?" Cam asks, coming to sit next to me. Am I?

"I'm exhausted."

━━━

7 months later...

When the fuck are they going to leave us alone?

"No, Officer, he hasn't made contact," Rowan informs them for the hundredth time. "He killed people I care about and stole my child. Do you think I'm protecting him?" she growls.

I'd burned the evidence of Jaxson Wheeler's true identity.

Serial killer.

The thought of Rowan ever finding out the extent of the dark monster's thirst inside her dad is unbearable. She'd break, and I'd never be able to put the pieces back together.

She worries constantly about her dad coming for Erica. Any sound, knock at the door, has her startling and racing to pick up the baby.

She was home a day before she moved the baby into her room, then both of them into mine.

We've become a unit. A baby machine. A family.

I know I'll have to rid the world of Jaxson Wheeler, though. He won't stay gone. Like me, hc loves something too precious to stay away from.

But she's not his. She's mine. And I'll do anything to

keep her safe—and that means killing him.

———

Entering Dr. Winters' office, she smiles at me and hands me an envelope.

"What's this?"

"A birthday card."

"Isn't this crossing some kind of ethical line?" I take the card from her and place it on the table.

"It's not every day you turn eighteen."

"Does this mean I can stop coming here now?" I sit back and lift my ankle to rest on my knee.

"Unfortunately, for your eagerness to get rid of me, you agreed to thirty months."

I know I don't have to stick with the terms. I'm eighteen now. I could tell her to eat shit and walk out of here never to return, but that's what she expects me to do, and if I'm honest, coming here helps me. It makes me feel normal. How fucked up is that?

"How are things at home?" she asks, picking lint

from her pant leg. It's the first time I've ever seen her legs covered.

"Great."

"How are the dynamics now?"

She wants to know if I've pursued things with Rowan. I planned on bottling those emotions and urges and burying them deep so I could be what she needed right now, but it's Rowan who's become needy for more.

Little looks she gives me of longing. The need to be held and always looking for my approval.

We're a team with Erica, like any other young couple with a baby you'd see, only we don't fuck.

"I think my brother is gay."

Winters can't mask her shock at this announcement. She drops the pen she's holding, then flusters to pick it back up.

"Camden?" she finally squeaks out.

"No, Brock."

"Why would you think that. Has he confided in you?"

"No."

I saw him and Ethan having a heated discussion, and it wasn't just friends having a falling out. There was passion and pain in their tone, posture, eyes.

"Have you asked him?"

I shrug. "It's none of my business."

"So why bring it up?"

To get you off the subject of Rowan.

TWELVE

R O W A N

2 months later...

#11 Trait of a Psychopath

Need for power

NINE MONTHS OLD, AND MORE ADORABLE WITH each passing day.

"Time for sleeps," I tell her, stroking her head and laying her down in her crib. I still can't bear to move her into her own room, so she's still in the room with Nixon and me.

When he moved my bed in here, he had to get himself a twin bed because the two queens took up too much space. I smile at the thought of everything Nixon does to make us comfortable and safe.

The light voices from downstairs travel up to us, so I close the door, put on Erica's nightlight, and begin her bedtime song.

"Twinkle, twinkle little star,

How I wonder where you are,

Up above the world so high,

Like a diamond in the sky,

Twinkle, twinkle little star,

Look down on us from where you are."

Taking her monitor, I come downstairs just as Nixon is getting home. The place is buzzing with bodies for a get together Hayden's having.

I look down at my jeans and blouse and cringe. There's a little bit of spit up on my shoulder. I'm underdressed compared to the glamorous dresses and suits the guests are wearing.

His get togethers have changed dramatically over the last year.

Nixon's eyes find mine through the crowd, and I smile when I see him in jeans and a T-shirt. The crowd parts for him like he has a force field around him, pushing them to move.

He commands any room he's in, even wearing casual attire.

Licking his lips, his gaze moves from my eyes to my mouth, and I try to ignore the pounding of my heart and the dull ache forming in my gut.

Things have changed so much between us. It's like we're dancing around this tension sizzling between us.

I'm too scared to make a move in case it's all in my head and he's just being Nixon, my best friend. Every instinct tells me it's so much more, but if I ruin this by making such a huge error, I wouldn't survive it.

He's become my oxygen. I need him.

"How did she go down?" he asks, rubbing his thumb over the milk spit up on my shoulder. I hand him the monitor and watch the dazed effect take over his features.

I've never known anyone to bring Nixon Pearson to his knees like Erica can. She has him wrapped around her tiny baby finger, and I feel sorry for anyone who ever makes her unhappy. His love for that girl is fierce, and he has three brothers all standing in line to protect her, heart and soul.

"I should go give her a kiss goodnight?" He poses it as a question, but we both know it doesn't matter what I say. He's going to kiss our baby goodnight.

"You look beautiful by the way. Haircut?" he queries, reaching around me to take a breadstick from a buffet of food laid out behind me.

Just one more thing I love about this boy. He notices small things and always knows when I need a boost. "Just showered." I bite my cheek and hide my embarrassment by looking away from him.

His fingers grasp under my chin, tilting my head to look up at him.

"Want to order some food and go watch a movie?"

I love him.

"There's tons of food. We can just take some of this."

Raising a brow, he looks over the buffet and shakes his head.

"Rowan, I'm eating a breadstick right now. A fucking breadstick. Because all that fish in shells crap looks like baby vomit."

A laugh rumbles up my chest. "They're oysters. They're supposed to be an aphrodisiac..."

Silence.

We're both just staring at each other, my cheeks turning pink and stomach knotting.

"Wouldn't be the first time I've tasted baby puke." He winks, grabbing a plate and loading it up before taking my hand and leading me upstairs.

The movie room has become a sanctuary of sorts for us. We like spending time in here, and with having a baby, I don't like leaving her, so we don't get to go to the actual theater.

Before I had Erica, that was something Lucy and I used to do together, but ever since my dad hurt her, neither the boys nor Trevor like us doing things alone, because my dad is still out there.

Thoughts of him linger in the back of my mind like a boogeyman under the bed.

My emotions were always conflicted over him, but after what he did to Lucy, and with no reason as to why, it's just left me hating the DNA running through my veins.

"I'm going to take a quick shower. Go pick something to watch," Nix tells me, placing our plates down.

"Okay."

My entire body is hyperaware of him, even a subtle brush of his skin with mine as he passes me nearly makes me groan.

Damn, I need some alone time to get myself under control.

I scan some of the new movies he's added and pick

something light and funny to try to get my mind out the gutter and cool my skin.

The smell of the puke on my shoulder makes me cringe. Dropping the remote on the chair, I race to our room, whip my top off, and rummage through the dresser to find one of Nixon's baggy tees to put on. The shower turns off, and I panic. I quickly pull the shirt on and end up with my head in an arm hole. As the door opens, the rest of the shirt is around my neck, leaving my bra-covered breasts on display, but that's not what has my cheeks setting a fire blazing down my neck.

Nixon is completely naked.

Flesh...all of it...just...right there. "I...erm...oh...erm," I stutter.

"There were no towels." He doesn't cover his junk with his hands. Instead, he stares into me, not at me.

My teeth sink into my lip, and I tug the shirt off my head, but don't make a move to put it on. We stare at each other as his cock thickens. That's all the invitation I need.

Because I've needed him for too long.

When I drop the shirt to the floor, he takes in a sharp intake of breath.

Yes. This is happening. I can't keep denying every moment I think about doing this with him.

I push my pants down in a brazen act, showing a confidence I don't feel.

My hand moves to cover the stretch marks on my lower stomach, but he puts his hand up, and whispers, "Don't."

I freeze, my bones solidifying, my chest moving rapidly up and down with my intake of breath.

"Don't ever cover yourself from me. You're the most beautiful thing I've ever seen."

This is Nixon and me. We've always had this chemistry between us, but now, it's evolved into so much more. I think when he actually touches me, I might combust.

"Take it all off, Rowan. Let me see you." It's a plea, not

a command, and my legs almost buckle at the desperation in his tone.

I reach back and unsnap my bra, letting it fall down my arms and to the floor.

His eyes rake over the newly exposed skin, and he swipes his tongue over his bottom lip, making my thighs squeeze.

"We're going to wreck our friendship," I warn, tucking my fingers into my panties and trailing them down my legs.

"We're just improving it, strengthening it, completing it."

He moves then, his strides eating the small space between us, until there's only a tiny gap keeping our bodies from being consumed by the other. He grasps the back of my neck, pulling me to him, and his lips crash against mine as my pelvis tilts upwards, needing contact with his. My breasts brush against his chest, the aching need hardening my nipples, our contact igniting what's become undeniable. We're made to be together. Nothing before this matters. We're the now—the forever.

It's everything.

E. V. E. R. Y. T. H. I. N. G.

Our movements are in sync, like we've been doing this our entire lives. His tongue moves against mine, tasting every part of mine.

We duel and dance, his hands moving to my hips and lifting me so I can wrap my legs around his waist.

A gasp sounds from my lips as his cock makes contact with my slit.

Skin on skin.

Flesh to flesh.

Soul to soul.

His hands take command, caressing my skin in ownership.

His teeth nip and bite as his tongue flutters over my skin, trailing kisses down my neck.

His grip on my body is bruising, and I can't get

enough. Grinding my hips against him, I moan and beg for him to take us all the way.

Gripping me closer, like he can't get close enough, like his body is trying to absorb my own, he takes us to the bed and sits down with me on this lap.

He smells of the forest after a rainfall, and I'm intoxicated by him.

I lick and caress his neck with my lips, tasting him. I never want to stop.

Strong palms move down to my ass, and he hesitates, resting his forehead against mine.

"You sure you're ready for this, Ro? Because once you're mine baby, you're mine forever."

"I've always been yours," I breathe, lifting my hips and sinking down onto this cock.

We both let out a harsh exhale, and then groan into each other's mouths.

We fit like we were created for each other, his girth stretching me just right before the point of pain.

I flex my hips and swallow his moan. He meets my movement with deep strokes of his own.

Everything else disappears, and all that's left is him and me, creating music with our panting. I drag my body over his, over and over, slow and deep, a dance of two souls.

"Why did we wait so long?" I groan, twisting my hips. He controls my movements while his mouth devours my nipples.

"Because you didn't know then."

"Know what?" I murmur, my muscles tightening as deep pleasure rolls through me in waves of euphoria.

"Know you belong to me, and I to you."

THIRTEEN

N I X O N

#12 Trait of a Psychopath

Lacking Empathy

PLANNING A ONE-YEAR-OLD'S BIRTHDAY PARTY HAS had Rowan stressed out.

"She won't even remember this," Camden tells her when one of the number "one" balloons pop.

"It will be on film forever, Cam. Forever means it has to be perfect."

Holding up his hands in surrender, his eyes expand as he backs away from momma bear.

"Damn," Hayden says coolly. "Can you imagine when Erica starts school, learns to drive, tries to get a boyfriend?"

I dig him in the arm with a hard punch. "Ouch, what the fuck?"

"She's never dating." I glare.

He snort-laughs. "I said tries to get a boyfriend." He pats his hand on my shoulder and goes to help Brock hang the banner.

"Oh no!" Rowan screeches.

"What is it, babe?" I move her hair off her shoulders and rub them firmly, smiling when she sighs into my touch.

"I left one of Erica's presents at Lucy's."

Lucy arrived already. My eyes search the room for a very pregnant, Lucy and kiss Ro's cheek. "I'll go get it."

She turns on her heel and throws her arms around my neck. "I love you. Have I told you that today?"

Burrowing my nose into her hair, I whisper into her ear, "Twice this morning with your orgasms."

Her little intake of breath makes my dick harden, and I debate whether we could sneak off for another round, but there's too many people here, and I have a present to pick up.

I slap Ro's ass with a love tap and make my way over to Lucy, who's sitting on Trevor's lap, his arm curled around her protruding bump, protecting their baby growing there.

"Lucy, Rowan left a present at your place. Can I run over and pick it up?"

Her face collapses, and she holds up her hand. "Shit, I wrote that down and still forgot to bring it."

There's ink scribbled on her palm, and I bite back a smile when Trevor rolls his eyes. I remember the exhaustion stage of pregnancy.

She rummages in her purse and hands me a set of keys that have about twenty keyrings attached, including mini pom poms.

Trevor shakes his head and pushes her hand down, handing me his keys instead.

"Pull into the garage and use that entry to gain access

to the main house. The gates will open automatically if you take her car, which is blocking the drive anyway."

Trevor grins devilishly. I separate the blinds to peek out and groan.

"You think a pink car bothers me?" I raise a challenging brow.

"Thousand dollars says you move her car and take your own."

"Ohhh," Lucy chortles.

I snatch the keys and shout out to Ro, "Uncle Trevor is adding an extra grand to Erica's savings."

Her car might be pink, but it has tinted windows, and it's a five-speed, which is just badass.

It takes twenty minutes to get across town to their new digs. Trevor freaked out when Jaxson got inside last time and insisted on a security gated house. The gate is ajar when I arrive, fully opening once I turn in toward it. The hairs on the back of my neck stand on end when I look around and see a black truck parked on the street a few houses up.

No one parks on the street in this area. The driveways are miles long, there's no need to.

The garage door lifts as I drive toward it, the computer system reading the license plate. I pull in and sit for a few seconds. Do I call Trevor? The police? Would Jax come here after being gone for a year?

I pull my cell out and call Hayden.

After a couple rings, his voice booms down the line, like he's trying to talk over the noise.

"What's up, bro?"

"Hey, is Trevor going out of town tonight?"

Silence, and then, "Weird fucking question to ask, but as it happens, yeah. We have some business on the east coast and he's the only one who can deal with this client. Why?"

"No reason." I hang up and wrap my hands around the steering wheel squeezing.

My heart pounds heavy in my chest and a rush of adrenaline courses into my veins.

Motherfucker. He's back for Lucy, and then who's next? Erica? Rowan?

No. Fucking no.

I open the car door and look around the garage for anything I can use as a weapon.

Trevor is too fucking neat. This place has everything locked in cabinets. Fuck. I'll have to use my own body strength to overpower him if he's in there. I've grown a lot since our last throw down. I have a lot more to lose than him, which gives me reason to overpower him. End him once and for all.

Using the keys, I unlock the door and step inside, my senses on high alert. I'm going to feel pretty stupid when I get inside here and there's nothing but my own paranoia for company. Creeping forward, I come through to their kitchen.

Da dum, da dum, da dum.

My heart pounds.

"You're not who I was expecting." As if my own thoughts summoned the devil himself, a shadow appears from behind me and his words cause a chill to race up my spine. I don't get time to react before he shoves me forward.

He's still a strong sonofabitch. Turning to face him, my eyes hone straight in on the needle in his hand.

"I bet. Have something planned for just the two of you?" I nod toward his hand.

"She's pregnant, you know," I snap.

His face falters. He didn't fucking know. I use the distraction and go at him. He's taken off guard. I hit him with a closed fist across his jaw and reach for the needle with the other hand in quick, precise movements.

I snatch it from him and jab it in his neck before he has a chance to recover or stop mc.

"Why?" he chokes out, his hand going to the entry wound.

He stumbles forward, but this shit is good and works fast. He falls, hitting the floor with a sickening thwack.

His eyes widen, and his hand twitches, reaching up toward me before falling back down, like it's too heavy to hold.

"Because I can't take the risk for you coming for what's mine," I tell him honestly. This is the last thing I want to do, but he would never just stay away.

I leave him there to contemplate while I set the place up for an end Rowan will be able to move on from.

Then, I'll pack up the present Rowan left here and return to my girls.

——FOURTEEN

J A X O N   W H E E L E R

STARING UP AT THE WHITE CEILING I TRY TO MOVE my arms but they don't move. I know they won't, I designed this drug this way for a reason but the instinct to survive is strong inside me and I clench my jaw and try harder.

Sounds of Nixon moving around opening and closing cupboards alert me to the fact he's still here and hasn't yet called the police.

I came here for my sweet Lucy. I'd managed to stay away for some time but coming back here to leave a birthday present for my granddaughter got me reminiscing about what I had to give up last time I was here.

A quick call to Four Fathers Freight and the secretary

was all too helpful informing me Trevor was out of town tonight and I could send the delivery I lied that I had, direct to his home address. She reeled it off even going as far as spelling the street name out like I had a low IQ.

It was too easy. Fated I thought.

And maybe it was fated, just not for the reason I wanted.

Maybe this was Nixon's fate, his role in my life. Not to be like me but to stop me.

Now my own poison is coursing through my veins and the green eyes of a boy I could have killed twice over is now leaning over me, my future in his hands.

"You should have stayed the fuck away," he tuts.

I want to tell him he knows that would never happen. I'm pulled here by the blood that runs in the veins of a girl he loves. My daughter Rowan.

She's finally with the right man. A man worthy of her. Look at him. He took me down, of all people. I'm a god amongst mortals. It took me years to hone my calm but Nixon is already years ahead of me.

"I'm pretty sure what you had in mind tonight, Jax, but I'm afraid I can't let you go through with it. Lucy is too close to Rowan, to us," he tells me. No strain or conflict in his tone.

Slipping his hands under my armpits he begins dragging me backwards through some double doors and lays me next to a table and chairs.

He moves out of sight but continues to talk.

"Rowan's happy, she's finally fucking happy and I can't let you change that."

Happiness is something I should want for her. Every feeling in my bones tells me I want vengeance, retribution for what was taken from me including Rowan. She allowed Eric to seduce her and she chose him over me. The killer inside me wants her to pay in blood but my willpower is stronger than the urges.

Rowan is my daughter, so I fight the need to snuff her out. I raised her, gave her everything, it would be a shame for all that to be gone with her pulse in a blink of rage.

"It's strange because I know what you are and I used to think we were the same." Nixon grunts from somewhere to my right. He sounds strained like he's doing hard labor.

"But were nothing alike. You kill people for satisfaction. A sexual thing," he puffs out, coming back into view. "I kill for necessity, to keep people I love safe."

What the fuck is he talking about. Kill? Who has he killed?

He once again grabs my underarms and swivels my numb body until I see a noose come into view. It's hanging from a light fixture on the ceiling. You're going to kill me? Fucking ME? I want to roar.

But my lips won't move.

"I know what you're thinking."

I doubt it.

"But that *will* hold your weight. You see there's wooden beams put in especially, because Lucy wanted some artsy fartsy chandeliers, that weigh the same as a small rhino." He reaches up grabbing the noose and pulls it down pushing it over my head.

Don't! I shout over and over in my head as he begins pulling on the extending rope and my body begins to shift upward.

His muscles bulge as he growls using all his strength to hike my body up. The rope is digging into my skin and I can feel it cutting, thanks to my designer drug. It numbs the motor and muscle function but doesn't stop the sensation of feeling touch; it's how I wanted it so my girls can feel me on them, in them.

My fucking head is going to pop right from the shoulders before he has me suspended up there.

Stop. Stop. Stop.

My feet hit a chair and my body tilts back and forth on it, I have no control to grasp purchase.

A chiming sounds and Nixon begins tying the rope around the handles of the double doors he pulled me through.

"Hang tight a minute," he jests, smirking and pulling his cell phone out his pocket.

"Baby, I hit traffic."

"Nix," Rowan breathes through loudspeaker. She sounds panicked.

"What is it?" His eyes clash with mine narrowing accusingly.

"Someone left a dollhouse on the back porch." She sobs.

"It's okay, baby."

"No. it's not. It's my dad. It has to be. Oh God, he's going to take her isn't he?"

"Over my dead body, baby." *Or yours*, he mouths silently at me with a pointed finger.

"Just come home, please."

"I'll be there soon, I promise...And Ro...I love you baby."

"I love you too."

He ends the call and shakes his head.

"This isn't how I wanted things to go, you just don't know when your time is done. You killed Eric, you got your revenge, but you just can't help yourself. Going to our house?" he grinds out.

"You signed you own death warrant. You knew what I was capable off, you saw it inside me and yet you pushed me to this."

A calm washes over me as realization dawns on me that I won't be leaving this house breathing. I've been bested by a boy, a fucking boy. I'm glad it's him. No one else is worthy of this honor and prison isn't something I'm made for.

It should be you. I want to tell him. Tell him it's ok, I understand, because I do. Rowan should be with a man who will kill for her. It's fitting, she was born in a pool of her mother's blood, death is her gift and curse.

"I'll look after them." He frowns, nodding his head. "I promise you that."

And then he boots the chair from beneath me.

My vision blurs and water builds in my eyes. I can't breathe, my instincts try to gasp out and suck air into my burning lungs. I will my hands to reach for the rope but I can't do anything but feel my life fade. My lungs seize and darkness clouds my sight. I'm dying.

He killed me.

He fucking did it.

Nixon Pearson.

Son.

Father.

Protector.

FIFTEEN

B R O C K

WHEN NIXON CONVINCED LUCY TO STAY OVER, my feet itched to leave so we could come back here and have the place to ourselves. Ethan invited an old girlfriend over to join us but she won't be here until later.

Trevor gave me a key so I could come and go if and when I chose to—a place to escape the madness of our house and be alone with whomever I wanted.

Ethan doesn't even let the car roll to a stop before he's out the door and taking the steps two at a time to the front door.

"I say we get naked and hit the Jacuzzi," he shouts, unlocking the door and almost tripping over the doorstep.

"You want to start without her?" I grin, pulling my

t-shirt over my head and kicking off my boots.

"No harm in having a warm up." He licks his lips, pushes his jeans down his legs, and then startles. "Fuck. Fuck."

I follow his line of sight, my heart thundering in my ribcage.

"Motherfucker. Back up, Ethan. Call the police."

Jax Wheeler hangs from a rope in the middle of the dining room. A chair overturned beneath him, eyes bulging, skin blue.

After everything, he killed himself.

"Should we cut him down?" Ethan panics, pacing the foyer while on the phone.

"Fuck no. Don't go near him."

He deserved worse than this—more than this—but seeing him there dangling, his tongue hanging out his mouth, gives me a sense of peace. It's over.

EPILOGUE

R O W A N

Trait **NOT** of a Psychopath

Love

WAITING FOR ERICA TO COME THROUGH THOSE doors is the most tense I've ever been. Leaving her for her first full day of childcare was the hardest moment of my life.

"She's going to have had a ball," Nix reassures me, taking my hand in his and squeezing, his fingers curling around mine securely. Every day, I feel more loved, more safe, more alive with him.

We took the leap into each other fully and never looked back.

We've been through a lot, his father and mother's

murders, my father's suicide from the guilt of killing them and trying to harm Lucy, but he's never failed me— not once.

He's my forever. My and Erica's.

A beeping shrills, and my heart picks up its pace as the doors unbolt.

It's the most secure childcare out there. Video monitoring throughout, serving a live feed of our children for us to watch if we feel a need to. I won't tell Nixon that I watched it for two hours today.

The doors open, and I begin tapping my foot.

"Baby," Nixon chuckles. "She's going to be super excited to see you, and you'll wonder why you spent the whole day worrying."

I nod my head enthusiastically. "I know, I know. Oh, I forgot her balloon! It's in the car," I panic, looking back at the parking lot. I'd insisted on getting her a balloon to congratulate her on her first day. She's always had a thing for balloons since her birthday, and the woman in the shop snickered, thinking I was joking when I told her what it was for. But there was my man, stepping up and chastising her for being unprofessional, then going into a whole speech about a mother loving their child, and when she has a child, she can comment.

She could have had five kids for all he knew, but he has a sense for these things, and when Nix turns his attention on you, good or bad, you're rendered speechless.

Leaning down, he brushes his lips over my forehead and releases his grip on my hand. "I'll go get the balloon. She's going to love it, almost as much as I love you."

"Wow, that much?" I grin, shouting after him, ignoring the stares from the other parents. It doesn't go unnoticed by the men here that the women have all not so subtly followed my man with their eyes as he passes them.

Adulthood has been good to him. He's gained a few more inches in height and shoulder width. Damn, he's built like a Viking, and I can't get enough of him. I'm not even mad at them checking him out, because he's mine, and I can't blame them being drawn to him like a moth to a flame.

A chorus of chatter sounds just as the carers begin filing out with the children.

Searching every brown-haired girl, my stomach knots with anticipation of seeing my baby. I know my reaction to having to leave her is extreme, but I've lost so much in my life, I like to see, feel, and smell what's mine next to me all the time—grasp on and never let them go. But I never let that need stop Erica from being around other toddlers and experiencing life. Those are my issues, not hers.

Blue eyes find mine through crowd of parents gathered to collect their own children, and my heart settles and begins a normal rhythm.

Waving my hand, I expect her to come running at me with excitement, but instead, she's pouting searching the gathering of parents.

"Sweety?" I call out racing toward her, her eyes dart to something to her right, and a bright Erica smile spreads up her cheeks, and she takes off running unsteady on her feet.

"Daddy! Daddy!" she screeches. Nixon swoops her up into his arms and attacks her with kisses, the balloon bobbing around over their heads.

Placing my hands on my hips, I shake my head in disbelief.

"What about Mommy's hello," I pout.

Erica is Daddy's girl, no doubt about it, and Nix has always given her a daddy and so much more.

When she first called him Daddy, I dropped to my knees and sobbed. We had always called him Nixy, but after spending a couple hours a day in daycare, she just came out and called him Daddy one random Thursday afternoon.

Seeing all the other children using that term for the men taking the role as the daddy in their lives, she just decided that was Nix to her and she never stopped since.

The other Pearson boys were beaming with pride when they heard Erica call him daddy in their presence. He earned that title, and we will never forget Eric, but we can't live in the past. Those ghosts don't haunt this family anymore. We're content, but more than that, we're happy and stupidly in love.

———

Nixon

Looking over at Ro, and then in the mirror at Erica, who's tapping at her balloon, I breathe easy and turn the car onto our old street. We moved out of the Pearson household over a year ago and into our own place, just the three of us, despite me trying to get Cam to come live with us. He refused, saying Hayden needed looking after. They moved out too, into a place more suited for two young men.

Ro draws my attention when she looks at her watch

for the fourth time since picking Erica up from daycare.

"Where are we going?" She widens her eyes as she takes in the scenery.

"A detour." I grin wickedly, knowing she'll be freaking out about missing her last class.

Little does she know, I've already arranged for Suzanne to pick up any school work she may need for the weekend.

Ro is in an incredible mother, but she's so much more than that, and not getting to go to college played on her mind. She didn't want any of her trust fund or inheritance, and wouldn't be content not earning her own money and having a career.

So, I enrolled her in college and paid her fees as a birthday present. She wasn't sure at first but the more we talked about it the more excited she became. She's studying interior design, and wants to open her own business when she graduates, with a loan from a very handsome benefactor who just happens to adore her.

This won't be a problem.

There are a lot of excellent business opportunities that lack the capital to even get off the ground. So I made a business out of starter companies. I make sound investments and give the little fish a chance to swim in the big pool.

"What the...?" Ro breathes as I pull up next to the plot of land that used to be both her house and mine.

Ro couldn't face ever going back to the house Jax raised her in. The yard held too many haunting memories, and my brothers and I all agreed our house was just a reminder of that time. It all needed to go—tearing down the old to move into the future burden free.

Opening the car door, I round it to get Erica out first, then open Ro's door.

Her mouth is hanging open, and a tear has fallen onto her cheek.

Using the pad of my thumb, I dab it away and take her hand in mine, helping her out.

Her eyes scan the space. I had a developer turn it into a rose garden. Ro always said she can't smell roses without thinking of Eric, so where his memory rests is now a huge array of colors. Clusters of every rose there is spouting up on every inch of the space that used to be her garden. Eric was a piece of shit, but we can't pretend he didn't exist. He's in us all in some way. And Erica should have a place to come.

A seating area and a tree is planted on the land that used to be our house, in respect of our mother. She may have had her issues but you only get one in your lifetime and she happened to be ours.

"I can't believe you did this," Ro breathes.

"This will always be here for you if you ever need to come or decide to bring Erica when she's grown."

She sniffles and turns away so Erica can't see her tears.

"Baby." I take both her hands in mine and turn her back to face me.

"This is our past, and that won't change, but you and Erica...you're my future—my always. It's always been you for me, Ro." I drop to my knee, and her eyes expand so wide, they make her other features appear tiny.

"Daddy?" Erica giggles.

"Come here, baby," I tell Erica.

I slip my hands from Ro's and pull a ring box from my jacket pocket, taking out the engagement ring for Ro and promise ring for Erica.

"Ro, I promise to always put you and Erica before any and everything else. I promise I'll never hurt you, never stop loving you, and never stop wanting you. Now and always."

Gentle sobs rattle Ro's petite frame as she looks down at the rings.

"Erica, I promise to be the best daddy you could ever want or need. I promise to keep you safe and never let you date. You are my forever and always, always."

I slip the ring on Erica's finger, and she beams at me,

holding the ring made of tiny little diamonds decorating the band.

"Ro, marry me, baby," I ask.

"Nix," she breathes. "You know we're going to wreck the friendship?" She sniffles and giggles at the same time.

I slip the ring on her finger.

"We're just improving it, strengthening it, completing it."

ENJOYED THIS BOOK?
MEET THE OTHER SONS

Four Sons Series by bestselling authors

J.D. Hollyfield, Dani René,

K Webster, and Ker Dukey

Four genres.

Four bestselling authors.

Four different stories.

Four weeks.

One intense, sexy,

thrilling ride from beginning to end!

These books were designed so you can read them out of order. However, they each interconnect and would be best enjoyed by reading them all!

A FOUR SONS STORY
There's a new sheriff in town...
HAYDEN
J.D. HOLLYFIELD

HAYDEN

BY JD HOLLYFIELD

I am a hothead, a wild card, and son to a murdered man. I crave the things I can't have and don't want the things I can.

Now, I'm left to pick up the pieces—stitch our family back together with a damaged thread.
This isn't the life I envisioned. And to make matters worse, the women in our lives are testing the strength of our brotherhood.

My name is Hayden Pearson.

I am the eldest—a protective, but vindictive son. People may think I'm too young to fill our father's shoes, but it won't stop me from proving them all wrong.

This series should be read in order to understand the plot.

A FOUR SONS STORY

Why choose one when
you can have both?

BROCK

DANI RENÉ

OTHER BOOKS IN THE
FOUR SONS SERIES

BROCK
BY DANI RENÉ

I am strong, athletic, and son to a man I always wanted
to be. I had made plans, thought I was on that path,
and then a bullet stopped not just my father's heart, but
mine too.

I've been living a life I'm not meant to.
I want more. I want to escape.
And I found someone who's given me a love I never
thought possible.

My name is Brock Pearson.

I am a free spirit who found happiness in an unexpected
place. People assume I'll be another heir to our empire,
but my heart belongs elsewhere.

This series should be read in order to understand the plot.

A FOUR SONS STORY
A ring won't stop
the determined...
CAMDEN
K WEBSTER

OTHER BOOKS IN THE
FOUR SONS SERIES

CAMDEN
BY K WEBSTER

I am intelligent, unassuming,
and the son of two murdered parents.
I'm calculating, damaged, and seek revenge.

I'll do whatever it takes to further my agenda, even if it
means seducing my way into a bed I don't belong.
Anything to make the ones who've hurt me pay.

My name is Camden Pearson.

I am focused, fierce, and power-hungry.
The youngest of four brothers.
People assume I'm the baby, but I grew up a long time
ago.

This series should be read in order to understand the plot.

ACKNOWLEDGMENTS

Readers. Thank you the reader for demanding these sons getting their stories. I hope we gave you what you wanted. Nixon was so much fun to write.

Kristi, thanks for listening to me rant, you're my brain twin and I love you.

My family always sacrifice time with me so I can work on creating book babies, thank you for being patient, eating takeout when I'm too tired to cook for you. For wearing creased clothes because Ironing is a waste of life hours and for putting up with me wearing headphones for 80% of the day and making you repeat what you tell me at least three times before I listen.

These titles don't happen with just us so THANK YOU to all the below:

Editor: Monica, thanks for always making us better. You've become an intricate part of my process. Thank you.

Proof Arc readers: Thanks Teresa, and Allison, for your keen eyes and willingness to drop everything and read for me. You're support is invaluable.

Formatting: Dani René, thanks for making the pages pretty

Cover: K Webster. You covers blow my mind, my Nixon cover is life. Thank you.

Bloggers. We adore you for all your passion, time and help with sharing, reading and getting our work out there.

Authors friends: Thank you for sharing and caring. For letting us nip in your groups and share are stories with you and your readers, this is a family and I'm happy to be apart of it.

My group: (Dukey's darker souls) Thank you to my wonderful admin and incredible readers and friends. Thanks for being patient and letting me work. I can always come in group and feel like you guys are genuine and amazing.

PA: Terrie, Thanks for sorting the cover reveal and release for Nixon. You rock, woman.

ABOUT KER

My books all tend to be darker romance, edge of your seat, angst-filled reads. My advice to my readers when starting one of my titles... prepare for the unexpected.

I have always had a passion for storytelling, whether it be through lyrics or bedtime stories with my sisters growing up.

My mom would always have a book in her hand when I was young and passed on her love for reading, inspiring me to venture into writing my own. Not all love stories are made from light; some are created in darkness but are just as powerful and worth telling.

When I'm not lost in the world of characters, I love spending time with my family. I'm a mom and that comes first in my life, but when I do get down time, I love attending music concerts or reading events with my younger sister.

STALK LINKS

News Letter sign up
http://eepurl.com/OpJxT

Amazon Author Page
https://www.amazon.com/Ker-Dukey

Website
http://authorkerdukey.com

Facebook
https://www.facebook.com/KerDukeyauthor

Twitter
https://twitter.com/KerDukeyauthor

Contact me here
Ker: Kerryduke34@gmail.com

Ker's PA: terriesin@gmail.com

Empathy series

OTHER BOOKS

Empathy

Desolate

Vacant

Deadly

The Deception series

FaCade

Cadence

Beneath Innocence - Novella

The Broken Series

The Broken

The Broken Parts Of Us

The Broken Tethers That Bind Us – Novella

The Broken Forever – Novella

The Men By Numbers Series

Ten

Six

Drawn to you series

Drawn to you

Lines Drawn

Standalone novels

My soul Keeper

Lost

I see you

The Beats In Rift

Devil

Co-written with K Webster

The Pretty Little Dolls Series

Pretty Stolen Dolls

Pretty Lost Dolls

Pretty New Doll

Pretty Broken Dolls

The V Games

Vlad

Ven

Vas – coming soon

Four Fathers Series

Blackstone – Jessica Hollyfield

Kingston – Dani René

Pearson – K Webster

Wheeler – Ker Dukey

51950763R00122

Made in the USA
Lexington, KY
13 September 2019